CATERING TO THE ALIEN

BEASTLY ALIEN BOSS, BOOK 3

AVA ROSS

FOREWORD

A note to the reader.

If you found this book outside of Amazon,
it's likely a stolen/pirated copy.
Authors make nothing when books are pirated.
If authors are not paid for their work,
they can't afford to keep writing.

*For my mom who
always believed in me.*

*And for my dad.
I found your handwritten stories
among your things!
They're amazing.*

SERIES BY AVA

Mail-Order Brides of Crakair

Brides of Driegon

Fated Mates of the Ferlaern Warriors

Fated Mates of the Xilan Warriors

Holiday with a Cu'zod Warrior

Galaxy Games

*Alien Warrior Abandoned/
Shattered Galaxies*

Beastly Alien Boss

*Screamer Woods Shared World
Orc Me Baby One More Time*

Stranded With an Alien
Frost

You can find my books on Amazon.

CATERING TO THE ALIEN

It's the cooking contest of a lifetime.
I just need to avoid falling for a hot alien chef.

To raise credits for the local creature shelter, I enter Interstellar Chef. If I win? I'm awarded the catering job of a lifetime and prize money I can donate to the shelter. It won't be easy—contestants must prepare exquisite meals in dangerous alien locations and fellow chefs have been known to attack the others. Some competitors don't make it home alive.

All I have to do is avoid my stiffest competition, Thrombuka Nargoth, the brutishly handsome, golden-skinned alien who once left me stranded without my undies in a secluded hallway of a dive bar on Quazar 3.

Fraternization among the competitors is strictly forbidden, but the more I try to avoid Throm, the more I can't resist him. Soon we're stealing kisses away from the prying eyes of the camera bots. If we're caught, we'll get thrown off the show.

Fate has other plans, however, and soon I don't know what I'm fighting for most—the prize money for the shelter or a future with Throm.

Catering to the Alien is Book 3 in the Beastly Alien Boss Series. Each features an Earth woman hired for an off-world job who meets a gruff alien who can't resist falling for his fated mate.

1

WREN

"Someone's staring at you," one of my friends said, nudging her head toward a corner of the dive bar in Viskius, the biggest city on Quazar 3.

We sat at a high-top table, nursing the drinks we'd ordered when we arrived.

As one of the chefs on an interstellar cruise, I didn't often take advantage of the chance to visit one of the ports the ship docked into throughout the galaxy, but a few of my fellow staff members invited me to go with them to Quazar 3 on our night off.

I'd shrugged and hopped into the transport shuttle with them, planning to have a couple of drinks, then return to the ship. I was scheduled for breakfast duty, which meant I needed to hop out of bed at four o'clock sharp.

I started to turn to see *who* was looking, but Faliera hissed, her forked tongue flicking out. She laid one of her four hands on my arm. "Play hard to get. Play hard to get!"

"I *am* hard to get." Spontaneity was not my middle name. I dated, but only after checking out a guy's resume.

Well, not exactly. But I had been known to ask his friends about him before accepting a guy's invitation.

"If you look, you signal you're interested," Faliera said.

"Maybe I am?"

"He's still looking this way," Juliest said, followed by a high-pitched gurgling giggle. This ruffled the flaps on her neck gills and made her face turn scarlet.

"Oh, my," gasped Faliera. Her tail shot up toward her back, nearly hitting an alien walking past our table. "Don't look!"

I nudged aside the hovering drink menu that kept zooming in close to my face, suggesting I order another. "But you just said—"

"Shh." Her lavender eyes widened, and her voice dropped off to almost nothing. "He's coming this way."

Trying not to be obvious about it, I'd glanced around, spying a golden-skinned alien standing close behind me with a tusk-baring smile on his face that made my knees melt faster than biergart fat in a sizzling hot frying pan.

My gaze locked with his, and while I fumbled to find something witty to say, he extended his hand my way.

"Allow me to introduce myself," he said with a dip of his head. He wore his nearly white hair with pale lavender streaks secured at the nape of his neck. The thick strands dangled halfway down his back. His bronze horns coiled across the top of his head, the blunted tips nearly touching his shoulders. "I'm Thrombuka Durvanak Nargoth. Throm for short."

Who introduces themselves by using their complete name anymore? Still, he sounded sincere. And I was a sucker for guys with pale blue eyes and taller-than-my-five-ten muscular frames, let alone tusks and horns.

"Can I buy you another drink?" he asked, nudging his chin to my nearly empty glass.

"Sure." I practically breathed the word. I could barely think with his skin touching mine.

One of the other women tittered.

I swallowed and tried to come up with something intelligent to say. Now would not be a good time to ask him for references.

He hailed the hover-menu and put in our order. "While we wait, would you like to dance?"

Dance? "Oh, um, yeah." I stood, and he kept hold of my hand, leading me out onto the dancefloor, a scrap of pleenar wood with barely enough room to sway around on.

Since he was at least a head-and-a-half taller than me, he lifted me up to bring me to eye level. My feet dangled. The only way to make this work was to wrap my legs around his waist and grab onto his shoulders. This should've put me well above anything hard down south unless the guy was big and long.

My eyes popped when I felt something shifting against my groin.

He shot me a grin, but when I spied a touch of shyness on his face, I relaxed. So he had a stiffy. That was a good sign, right?

We swayed around until the dance came to an end.

"Thanks," I said.

"Thank you." He grinned, and damn, tusks. I'd always wondered what it would feel like to kiss a guy with tusks.

With the light buzz from my first drink loosening my inhibitions, I decided to find out. I leaned forward and planted my lips on his. His tusks didn't hurt. In fact, they felt sensual rubbing against my upper lip

I'd read about heat searing through a woman's veins, of

being suddenly desperate to be with someone from one touch alone, and of aching to rip off clothing to feel skin on skin.

No one had brought this out of me until I kissed Throm.

I had a feeling I'd been missing out on all the fun stuff.

In seconds, we'd left the dance floor. He carried me down the hall, his lips still locked on mine.

I groaned and rubbed against him, not caring if my coworkers saw me. Not caring that I barely knew this brutish alien. I hadn't even quizzed one of his friends.

The back of the hall curved to the right, then dead-ended at a closet. With one big, clawed hand gripping my ass, he yanked the door open with the other and hauled out a lonely broom and mop resting against the back wall, tossing them onto the floor of the hallway.

We tumbled inside. The door banged shut as he pressed me against the wall, lifting me and grinding himself against me.

A fever charged through my cells, linking them together. Nothing would satisfy me other than feeling his long, thick, glorious cock buried deep within me. Whimpering, I tore at his clothing while he yanked down my pants.

"Bend forward, luscious," Throm growled, pivoting me around. "Your lips are sweeter than hoolig, and I need a taste of everything else you have to offer."

"Someone might see," I said, heat climbing into my cheeks. Truly, though, did it matter? He'd kissed me out of my inhibitions, my undies, and my willpower. There was nothing stopping him from claiming me other than his dark leather pants.

He leaned me forward and stooped down between my legs, parting my thighs. I was dripping already.

Someone knocked on the door, the sound barely breaking through my overwhelming lust.

"Ignore it," I cried, shimmying closer to his face. I'd sacrifice anything to feel his tongue gliding inside me.

He stood and cracked the door, shielding me from view with his body, and spoke to whoever stood on the other side in a tone too low for me to hear what they said.

Throm shut the door. Frustration gleamed in his eyes, and his hard cock kicked against the front of his pants. "I'll be right back."

"What?" I asked.

"Hold that pose," he said with a low, husky chuckle, stroking my bare ass with a claw. "I promise. I won't be long."

He slipped out of the closet.

And that was the last time I saw Thrombuka Durvanak Nargoth.

One Interstellar Year Later

"You're fired," my boss snarled, her four suction cup-covered limbs flailing in the air. One smacked on the grill and sizzled, but she was so angry, she didn't appear to notice. "If you will not work all night, you will leave the premises immediately."

I ducked to keep from being hit by one of her longer upper limbs. She wasn't vicious—not usually—but when she was pissed off, she could be unpredictable. There was no need for me to see stars after a blow to the head. Been there, done that once already. It sucked working with a blinding headache.

My boss was in an uproar because I'd refused to work when my shift was finished. I'd been here twelve hours already. Exhausted after working in the kitchen alone all day, my eyes stung, and my arms had turned into lead poles dangling at my sides.

"Please don't fire me," I said, struggling to sound reasonable. "Think of the creatures."

This was actually my second job. The first paid for my tiny room here on the space station and food/essentials. This part-time job generated a small check I donated each lunar cycle to the local creature shelter.

It was too common for ships to dock at the space station and dump the pet they'd brought with them. Like they thought someone would scoop the poor creature up and adopt them. Nope. I found many wandering the bowels of the station with hunger and desolation in their eyes. The shelter found them loving forever homes.

However, it wasn't easy to find decent chefs on a space station. My boss needed me more than I needed her.

She pressed her flat, gray face close to mine. "If you do not—"

My com chimed, and with relief flooding me, I held up my arm to show her I had a call.

She snarled and snapped but backed away.

I ducked into the hallway outside the kitchen and leaned against the wall, blowing stray strands of hair off my face.

When my com chimed again, I clicked into the message.

You, Wren Phillips, have been chosen to compete in the next round of Interstellar Chef!

Wait, what?

My eyes widened as I verified what I'd heard with the text. This must be a mistake. Sure, I'd applied for the position at the Interstellar Employment Agency on a whim a lunar cycle ago, but I never dreamed I'd be selected.

You will compete with four other contestants, the shrill, accented, alien voice said through my com. *The person with the lowest score each day will be eliminated from the show, and whoever wins the final round will cater the reception for the upcoming wedding of Crown Prince Lordenfeer and his illustrious Earthling bride.*

Everyone had heard about the prince and the Earth woman he'd met at the palace. Their wedding would take place in one lunar cycle. Whoever scored the catering job would be inundated with job offers from restaurants. But with the prize credits, the winner could open their own business.

This couldn't be happening. It was the chance of a lifetime. There wasn't a chef in the galaxy who wouldn't leap at the opportunity to compete on Interstellar Chef. The show was recorded and streamed throughout the multiuniverse. Even the losers often received offers of employment.

Yeah, the show was purported to be dangerous, but surely everyone made it home alive. The "deaths" were staged. Right?

With the prize, I could finally leave the space station and start over in a place where my mother's shadow didn't hang over me. Just as exciting, I could donate to the creature shelter, and they'd be financially set for years.

Please confirm your receipt of this offer and interest in participating in the show, the alien voice said through my com. *And then prepare yourself to be transported to the Bressarian Arena for the opening event tomorrow. Since space is tight on the shuttle, you may only bring one bag. Outfits emblazoned with the show's logo will be provided for each of the events. Pack light! Pack well. And get ready for the cooking contest of a lifetime!*

Receipt confirmed, I'm in. I typed with shaky fingers. *I want to participate,* I added in case "I'm in" wasn't clear.

My heart zinged around, smacking against my ribcage. I couldn't believe it. It was all I could do not to cry.

Hey, it was time to start packing.

Well, I'd pack as soon as I finished up here.

Your transport will arrive at the space station's dock X37 to collect you promptly at 08:00 tomorrow morning. We wish you all the best in the competition.

My com bleeped as the transmittal cut out.

I danced around the hall, giggling madly.

"I'm going to win this," I kept singing.

"There you are," my boss bellowed, snaking her limbs through the kitchen doorway. Two latched onto me, and I was lifted off the tile floor and hauled into the sweltering, grease-scented room. "Get to work or you're fired." She smacked me down in front of the grill hard enough my teeth jarred together.

"You can't fire me," I said with quiet dignity. "Because I quit." I wrenched off the stained apron I'd worn since that morning while preparing delicate cuisine and tossed it at my boss. "Send my final check to the creature shelter."

She deflected the apron with a snap of a limb and stomped toward me on her four hooves. "Get out of my kitchen," she snarled.

"Alrighty, then." I lifted my chin and resisted taunting her with how she'd never find another chef who could match my delicate sauces, how she didn't know the secret ingredient I included in my fry batter, and how she had no clue how to prepare a tuskareen roast so that the meat melted off the bone.

With a big grin, I stomped from her kitchen.

Three days later, I stood in a small room at the top of the floating Bressarian Arena, fidgeting while I waited for my name to be announced for the upcoming season of Interstellar Chef.

Sweat trickled down my spine, and I wiggled in the stupid, form-fitting sparkly silver gown they'd asked me to wear for my introduction.

The arena orbited one of the small moons of Quazar 3. I hadn't returned there since the cruise, and I cringed at the idea of walking through the streets of Viskius City again.

After Throm had bailed on me, I'd pawed around inside the broom closet, but my panties were nowhere to be found. Had Throm taken them with him? Jerk.

I'd hurried back to my friends; told them I had a headache—which I totally did—and returned to the cruise ship.

I'd given my notice the second the ship put into the space station.

At least I didn't have to go anywhere near the bar. I'd leave the arena for the first event that would take place on Trillaphon in the Wondron Sector, along with the other four competitors.

A tall, blue-skinned female who'd earlier introduced herself as Trixaine opened the door and poked one of her two small heads inside the opening. A grin split her face, stretching from one cheekbone to the other. "Are you ready, honey?" She curled one of her three fingers my way. "It's time."

I followed her from the room, my impossibly high heels clicking on the floor and the hem of my gown swishing across my ankles. I wouldn't compete in this outfit, thank the stars. Matching tunics and pants with the show's logo emblazoned across the front would be waiting in my shuttle cabin.

I felt like a thick knife. Or a silver torch. Watchers were going to be blinded by my stunning appearance—literally.

"So, honey," Trixaine said, her two heads undulating, softly bumping against each other. Her snake-like hair had been coiled up on the top of each of her heads with a gold chain linking the braids in the back. Her thick, scaled tail swayed back and forth, bumping into the walls of the narrow hallway. "When you get out there, they'll ask you some basic questions." She flashed her fangs. "Nothing too personal. This will give you a chance to show the multi-universes who you are. It's your time to shine."

As I stood beside her, cheers erupted from the arena, followed by clapping.

I sucked in a deep breath. "What should I expect out there?"

"You'll step onto an orbiting island. It will transport you up beside our very own Jell Pleecard, the Bretak nobleman who will host the season."

I'd met him this morning when he stopped by my cabin.

"He'll ask you a few very easy questions," Trixaine said. "Relax and try to sound natural when you give your answers. After that, you'll be introduced to the other competitors."

I released a heavy breath. "Good. It sounds simple."

She wrapped an arm around my shoulders and

squeezed so tight I almost yelped. "Very simple. No fear. No worries. This is going to be a lot of fun."

Cooking was fun. An introduction being live streamed to trillions of aliens throughout six or eight universes?

Major cringe.

I didn't enjoy being stared at, though I supposed I'd have to get used to it since I'd be under the scrutiny of the camera bots for the next week or so, other than during my free time.

I braced myself and nodded. "I'm ready."

The door opened, and I stepped out onto the orbiting island. I was lifted until I reached the center of the enormous arena. I'd expected stands with beings watching the opening event, but only a ton of hyper-link camera bots floated around, taking everything in from all angles.

"Welcome," Jell cried, zooming in close to me. Hover jets had fused with his lower legs, and I'd read he wore them almost all the time. "May I say, Wren, that dress looks fabulous on you. You shine!"

"Thank you," I said in the lull that followed.

Cheers erupted, making me jump, and I realized they were fake, injected into the show to make viewers believe a billion aliens were watching.

"Without further ado, let's get started, shall we?"

I pressed for a grin, but it came out weak.

"What is your favorite food?" Jell asked, nodding his head in an encouraging manner. "Just speak normally, dear. The camera bots will hear you just fine."

"My favorite food?" I said, my spine loosening. Maybe this wouldn't be too bad. The lack of audience made my spine loosen and my frayed nerves unravel. "Jujist berries."

"Ah, lovely. And spices." He wiggled the spikes on his

shoulders. "Here's a tricky question. What spices would you use to enhance a limerund roast?"

My smile came easier. "Everyone knows a limerund roast is best seasoned with cardira."

"No," he gasped in mock excitement, two of his four hands cupping his bright pink cheeks. All of him was pink, actually—the parts I could see outside of his deep purple suit. "But cardira is sweet."

"Garlic and a touch of dundun cut the sweetness. It's amazing." I grinned. "You should try it sometime."

"Oh, you can be assured, I will!" His gaze moved to the closest camera bots. "Did you hear that, folks? Cardira and dundun. *Ahh.*"

A fake cheer and applause rang out while he nodded approvingly, flashing his three-inch fangs.

He asked me six more questions, each designed to make me look good. I knew this because they were all as easy as the first. I was soon relaxed and almost enjoying my introduction. I could ignore the cameras and be myself.

"Thank you," Jell finally said. "We *all* thank you! I know our viewers will have more questions, and I'll happily collect and ply them at a later date. But for now, I ask you to wait with three of your fellow chefs while I introduce the last."

My island took me over to wait with theirs.

"And the final contestant is . . ." A drumroll sounded as Jell whizzed past us on his hover jets.

A hovering island rose from below like mine had, revealing a male dressed in tight black pants and a billowy white shirt.

My breath caught.

Throm's intent gaze met mine.

2

THROM

I restlessly waited for my introduction, hovering on my island below the others. I'd listened with only half an hear as the first three competitors for this season's Interstellar Chef were quizzed.

I was most interested in the last.

This morning, when Jell stopped by to introduce himself, I'd seen the names of the other competitors on his telescreen.

Wren Phillips was a common enough name.

But I knew in my heart it was *her*, the pretty, luscious little human I'd nearly had sex with.

I hadn't seen her since I left her in the broom closet at that bar on Quazar 3 to attend to an urgent matter. When I closed my eyes, I could still picture her sweet ass poking toward me. The heady feel of her lips beneath mine. The way she'd pressed her body against me with need.

The overwhelming longing roaring through me to claim her body and soul.

By the time I'd returned to the closet, she'd left. I'd been unable to find her, and no one in the bar could tell me where she'd gone.

I needed to make amends, but today, I was a competitor.

I needed the prize money desperately. Losing was not an option.

And fraternization among the competitors was strictly forbidden. I could be nice to Wren, assuming this was the same female. I could touch her hand in passing. But I was not allowed to take things any further.

This assuming she'd let me near her. She might smack me across the face when we met up again.

Or not. It had been an interstellar year. She may have forgotten who I was. Forgotten our kiss and what we'd nearly done in that closet.

"Allow me to introduce you to the final contestant of the season, Chef Thrombuka Durvanak Nargoth." As my floating island soared toward Jell, he batted his eyelashes, flirting with the camera bots. "I believe you prefer to go by Throm?"

I couldn't look anywhere but at *her*.

It *was* the pretty little human I'd met an interstellar year ago. The one I'd nearly had sex with.

My fated mate. I'd known it the second I saw her with her friends from across the bar.

I flashed Jell a grin, watching Wren glaring my way out of the corner of my eye. "I do prefer Throm, thanks."

"Allow me to introduce you to the other contestants, and then we'll get down to the questions," Jell said.

As my island passed the other contestants, I thrust out my hand, an odd, Earthling way of greeting someone. "It is nice to meet you . . . Omyn, Crik'ee, Aesoars, and Wren." My island waited in front of hers. "Wren is such an unusual name."

"Now, now," the announcer trilled, smacking my shoulder with a long limb. "No flirting. You know the rules."

She stared at my hand in disgust.

I deserved the look and the emotion behind it, but I couldn't explain why I'd left her with the multi-universes watching, eager to dissect our every word and action.

In fact, for both our sakes, it would be best if I didn't communicate with her at all.

I let my hand drop to my side. While the others had given me limp shakes, she wasn't going to do the same.

Their islands zipped backward to allow the spotlight to shine on me, and I turned back to Jell.

"Yes, well," he said in high cheer, sweeping his limbs out to draw the audience's attention. "Let me ask you a few questions, Throm. First, are you mated?"

What? I was told they wouldn't ask us anything too personal.

Jell smacked my shoulder again, and if he kept it up, I'd sock him.

"I'm a chef," I said. "I own a restaurant on my home planet of Aegrin. I date, though I haven't done that in . . ." I glanced at Wren who watched raptly. "In an interstellar year."

"Ah, so you *are* in the dating pool," Jell said. "Hear that, ladies and gents? Throm is available!"

Why would the audience care?

When I shot him a glare, he huffed but continued, thankfully keeping the questions to safer, less personal topics. I named my favorite spice and which sauce I preferred with muskileen fruit. Easy stuff and a way for the audience to feel a connection to the contestants.

"Very well then," Jell finished. "I'll send you over to join the rest of the group."

Now that I wasn't on display, I studied the other contestants, wondering who, other than me, stood the chance of claiming the final win.

Omyn, the male nearest to me, hailed from Sevest. When my floating island stopped beside him, he dipped one of his two heads forward. His six arms shifted along his sides, and his intent, orange eyes were also analyzing the competition. Wren specifically. As tall as me, his frame possessed about half my bulk. His comically big feet shuffled on the island, though anyone who pointed that out to one of his warrior race might soon wind up with his throat fileted open. Sevests did not enjoy being mocked.

Or losing.

Aesoars stood on the island beyond Omyn. Another male, he came from the planet Brevule. A highly peaceful race, Bervules had a strong sense of justice. He'd be an honest contestant, and he'd expect the same from us. I hoped his naïveté wasn't destroyed before the event was through.

The oils his blue skin secreted made him shine in the beams generated by the floating lights. He preened and waved to the audience, his big grin revealing long, pointy fangs.

Beyond him, I caught the solitary eye of Crik'ee, also a male competitor. They didn't select females for the show very often, a discriminatory policy. Wren was the token female added to placate those who complained.

Crik'ee's planet, Eiy'as, was located near the end of the most recently explored galaxy.

The Eiy'as preferred living in simple huts and maintaining the lifestyle they'd enjoyed for longer than anyone could remember, rather than adopting the sophisticated buildings and technology everyone else throughout the multi-universe had chosen.

It would be unwise to dismiss Crik'ee, however. He would be a formidable opponent, and not only because he could handle multiple tasks with his eight arms. His race was known for the delicacy of their dishes infused with robust flavors and spices. I envied those who'd get to sample what he'd made.

He caught my eye and nodded, his pale green lips twitching upward. High color suffused his darker green skin, and I assumed he was nervous. It must be hard being away from his home world for what I assumed was the first time.

"Now that we all know each other," Jell said. "It's time to . . ." His voice lifted into a screech. When he cut off, the fake audience roared. He smiled, baring his fangs. "Yes, it is time! Your shuttle has arrived, my lovely chefs. You'll now be transported to our very first destination, Trillaphon." He flew forward, his legs splaying out in excitement, and did a back flip before soaring back to hover in front of us. "Trillaphon is a glorious planet in the Wondron Sector, and I'm sure you'll be delighted to get to know it better."

Glorious and delighted were a stretch. From what I'd read, dense jungle covered the planet. We were expected to prepare a meal in a jungle? That would prove a challenge, which was the point of the show.

"While you travel, you'll enjoy the amazing cabins in your private shuttle," Jell said with glee.

That was an outright lie. From what I'd heard, our quarters were barely the size of an escape pod, and we'd be lucky if each of us was given a private room. Although Wren's odds, as the only female, were better.

"Once you arrive on Trillaphon, you'll be taken to the area where your cooking stations are set up. Be prepared," one of Jell's limbs swept past each of us, pausing to shake the tip in our faces, "because immediately after that, you'll be given your first cooking task!"

Each event involved preparing one meal, and it could be anything from breakfast to lunch, dinner to dessert, to appetizers and party food. We'd have to cook with a mystery ingredient, plus other offerings specific to each destination. The courses would be scored by judges, and at the end of the day, one chef would be booted from the show.

The winner of each event would receive a prize. Sometimes, they'd send a winner to a special location on the planet for one night; other times, the winner might receive a big bottle of local wine. I'd read they polled the audience to pick the prize.

"Ah, I've just been informed that the shuttle is here," Jell crowed.

I'd been too lost in my thoughts—and watching Wren for any sign her justified anger had softened—that I'd missed the arrival of the craft on the floor of the arena.

A platform extended from the shuttle. After our floating islands took us down to the lowest level, we strode on board.

Inside, the craft's single staff member indicated where each of us would sleep, surprising me when we got our own rooms. Mine held a large bed instead of the simple bunks I had seen on prior shows, a major upgrade.

The other three entered their rooms, closing the doors behind them.

Before Wren could step inside her own chamber, I tapped her arm.

"Could we speak for a moment?" I asked.

She glared at me, but her face smoothed when she noted the camera bots mounted in strategic locations along the hall. As part of the reality show, they'd film us everywhere except within our private quarters. They'd tried to showcase the inside of the rooms during the first season, but one time, they'd caught a contestant pleasuring himself. In another, the viewers complained about watching someone file and paint their claws. After that, they mostly stuck to the main events, other than now, when the audience would be greedy to see more from us before the first event.

"I don't believe we have anything to stay to each other, chef," she said, her voice holding notes of sarcasm.

I had a long, steep hill to climb before she'd forgive me—assuming she ever did.

"Please. I won't take much of your time. I'd like to strategize about the other contestants."

"Why?"

"Because we're allowed to do so."

She huffed, and her lips thinned. "All right."

She stepped inside, and I followed, shutting the door behind me.

"What do you want?" she snarled, reeling around to face me. Color rose into her medium tan cheeks, highlighting her dark blue eyes, and her glorious black hair streamed down her back. Just like the first time I saw her sitting on the opposite side of the bar, my heart stalled. It picked up to a jerky gallop, and the symbol on my right inner wrist burned.

Yup, even without the symbol that appeared when I

first touched her, there was no denying she was my fated mate.

"What do I want, Wren?" I growled. "You. I want you."

3
WREN

"Well, you can't have me," I said sharply. "You had your chance a year ago—*maybe*—and now it's gone." I jerked my hand toward the doorknob, determined to open the door and shove him out into the hall. Then I'd slam the door in his face. "Besides, we're not allowed to hook up even if I wanted to."

My jaw had dropped when he told the audience he hadn't dated in a year. I knew very well what he was implying, but I wasn't buying it for a minute. He'd probably screwed his way across the multi-universe since he bailed on me.

"At least you remember who I am," he said.

How could I forget? Backing away from him because he looked and smelled so good my knees had started shaking, I propped my knuckles on my hips and tried to look bigger. That's what birds did with predators, right? They fluffed their wings and hoped the hunter was frightened enough to back off. "I'm actually surprised *you* remember *me*."

"I'll never forget your ripe ass and how much I ached to taste what you hid between your thighs," he said. His lips twitched upward before smoothing. He was as cocky now as he'd been a year ago. Then, the words coming out of his dirty mouth had thrilled me. Now, they made me want to snarl.

"You were slick with the charm a year ago." I lifted my chin and sniffed. "Not so much now. You've lost your touch." Not really, but it was my turn to sound cocky.

He backed up to lean against the door, running his hand through the thick bands of hair draping off his head. He'd probably worn it down to impress the female audience. "So you admit I have charm."

"*Had* charm. I'm impervious to it now."

One side of his thick brow ridge lifted, shifting his golden, segmented skin. "Is that a challenge?"

The flash of his tusks made my heart speed up, but I stiffened my spine and my resolve.

"Why would you care?" I asked. "You took off, leaving me in a broom closet without my panties." I frowned. "Where are they, by the way?"

"You want them back?"

"Not if they've been in your possession for a year. Yuck."

He snorted. "You didn't find any of this yucky a year ago."

I sighed. This convo was going nowhere. "You need to leave my room. Pretend we never met. Treat me like the rest of the contestants."

"I intend to do that anyway. If you win, it'll be because your dishes score the most points solely on their merits."

"That's right. I'm going to win." Despite him acting in a jerkish manner a year ago, I was confident he wouldn't use what happened between us to take advantage of me. I wasn't sure why I was so sure about that, but I was. Perhaps my belief came from the steadiness in his pale blue eyes. Or his posture that, if I didn't know better, hinted at a touch of vulnerability. "Why *did* you take off?"

I hated that my voice came out soft. Defenseless. Just thinking about it made my chest start aching all over again. I'd spent a year cursing his memory. I should be long over him by now

"My sister was in a horrible accident," he said.

I blinked. When he left me without my undies, I hadn't expected he'd done so for a reason like this. "I'm sorry. Is she okay now?"

He nodded curtly. "She's better. She's had a lot of rehabilitation at a high cost."

"Is that why you entered? For money to help her?"

His easy smile slipped out, though sadness still haunted his features. "It's an honor to be asked to appear on the show, but yeah. I want her to have the best rehab possible."

"I'm glad you take care of her. Some people wouldn't bother."

He shrugged. "I can't do anything less. I love her."

And just like that, I forgave him. I wanted to cling to my irritation, to snap and snarl at him to get revenge for my hurt feelings, but how could I do something like that? He could've returned to tell me what was going on, but in his position, I'd only be thinking of my sister.

His hand jutted out. "Do we have a truce?"

Back in the arena, I'd scorned him, ignoring his hand. Conflict churned through me now. I wasn't all in; how could I trust him not to hurt me again if I let down my emotional guards? Besides, we were competing here, for heaven's sake. Only one of us could win.

"How do you feel about losing?" I asked him.

He chuckled. "I could ask you the same thing." His hand never wavered.

"I don't lose."

"I don't either."

"Then it's a draw."

He shrugged. "I believe so."

I wasn't one to hold grudges. We could be friends. There was no need to do anything that might cost me more panties.

After hesitating a second, I took his hand and squeezed his so-much-bigger-than-mine fingers. "We have a truce."

"Good," he said, flashing his tusks again.

Yeah, knees, get a grip.

"May the best chef win," he said.

"That would be me," I quipped, though I laughed through the words. Something about him made my bones giddy, and I didn't like it, because it made me want to fling myself into his arms.

"We'll see about that, won't we?" He turned and left.

I sagged against the back of the door, shoving my hair out of my eyes.

This was going to be an interesting competition.

4
THROM

I woke to the big bed buzzing beneath me.

"Time to rise," a chipper, computerized voice called out. "The day has begun, and the show will start in less than two horus!"

Computers. I hated them. On my home world of Aegrin, I could sleep in as long as I liked. When my sister was hurt, I'd had to hire someone to manage my restaurant. I'd lucked into someone who could do the job as well as me. This freed me up to be there with my sister, to encourage her when she was down and push her when she gritted her tusks and gave it her all.

When I had time, I popped into the restaurant to prepare a few dishes.

I tossed back the covers and strode across the small room to the sanitizer, stepping inside and shutting the door. A small light bloomed overhead, and I stood still while the device cleansed my skin. It then coated me with a light emolument that would keep my segmented skin supple. It made me gleam more than I liked, but that was included at the insistence of the show's producers. The audience salivated over a "hot"—as they put it—chef, and who were they to deny the titillation of mine and the other males' exposed, gleaming bodies?

As for Wren, I'd heard a short skirt would show off her legs. If she were wise, she'd balk at the heels I'd heard they planned to leave in her room.

It really was a meat market in more ways than one.

As part of my instructions, I was told to strut about with my chest bare until it was time for me to start preparing food for the first event. They wanted a flash of skin, not to watch said skin burn.

A growl rumbled in my throat. I was no exhibitionist.

If I won, I'd have enough credits to settle my sister in her own home with state-of-the-art devices to aide her until she could do everything by herself. I visited her every chance I could, but she was lonely, and she missed our city and her independence. For now, I scraped together the credits to keep her in rehab.

Jenniska was my world. She had been since our parents died when she was three and me eighteen. I'd taken care of both of us since, going to school in the evenings, while working my days as a dishwasher while a neighbor watched over my sister. The owner of the restaurant must've seen promise in me no one else had, because he promoted me to junior chef and taught me everything he knew.

When he died, he left me the restaurant. I'd made plans to borrow against it to expand into other cities, but I squashed the idea when Jenniska was hurt.

I'd be grateful to him until my dying day because, without him, I wouldn't have been able to help my sister.

I dragged on pants and boots and left the room, meeting up in the hall with the other contestants.

Omyn's pale orange skin gleamed like mine, and he preened, thrusting out his chest when he saw me. I might be the only one who wasn't excited about showing off skin.

He sent me a sharp look, and I internally sighed, guessing he viewed me as his main challenge. Contestants had been known to do anything to ensure they won, be it disabling one of the others, sabotaging a plate ready to be judged, or using mind games to trick us into believing we'd lost already.

If I guessed correctly, he was already eager to establish dominance, a common trait for his warrior species.

I met his gaze with a lifted brow ridge and steel running down my spine. I'd stared down more than one head chef hoping to displace me while I trained with the restaurant owner.

Aesoars and Crik'ee shouldered each other good naturedly, joking about showing off skin and how they were going to outcook each other. At least they hadn't yet succumbed to the cutthroat attitude common in this competition.

Everyone went silent when Wren stepped out of her room.

From the moment I met her, she drew me in. Her bright smile, the cute way she'd danced. And her kiss . . .

I'd spent many nights lying in my bed, aching to feel her warmth beside me.

I was stupid to fall for someone so fast. Even stupider to abandon her in a compromising position. I'd had a good reason, but I'd hurt her.

She was as glorious and unobtainable as a meteor flashing across the sky.

I wanted a second chance, but with her as my competition and the no-fraternization rule, I couldn't ask for anything. Not yet.

I could only hope we'd come out of this without hating each other, another common occurrence in this show. One rival had killed another within a week of last season's show. I'd have to be wary, but of the three males, not Wren. I'd never believe her capable of causing me true harm.

Nothing would stop me from trying to convince her to see me after the show was over.

This time, I'd finish what I started in that closet an interstellar year ago.

Omyn watched her with a hooded, predatory gaze that made the flexible spikes on my spine twitch. In my species' past, I would've challenged him for looking at her like that.

Now, I had to behave. Mostly.

"Wren," I said, trying not to gnash my tusks. "Nice to see you this morning."

Aesoars and Crik'ee giggled in what I took as a mocking tone, but Crik'ee dragged his gaze away from mine fast.

When he turned his back on Wren, *slighting* her, I growled.

She lifted one delicate eyebrow his way and huffed. Striding past all of us, she headed for the front of the shuttle.

"We've landed," she tossed over her shoulder as the ship touched down and the engines unwound. "Time to get cookin'. Tell me, guys, whose ass am I going to whip today?"

My laugh shot out as I followed her.

I'd yet to taste her cooking, but her attitude and sharp wit couldn't be beat.

5

WREN

id Throm have to run around without a shirt on? The other guys . . .? Who cared about them? All I could see was Throm, larger than life and looking at me like he'd savor eating *me* for breakfast.

His black pants hung low on his narrow hips, and the heavy bulge in the front drew my eye. I shouldn't look.

And I sure shouldn't dream about what it would feel like to . . .

My growl slipped out. *Focus, Wren.* The other contestants were insulting me while I was salivating about Throm's ripped bod. He was the freakin' competition. I couldn't be distracted by his gorgeous physique.

Time to put a cap on my hormones until this show was over.

As for my other competitors, it figured I'd be matched with a bunch of jerks. While I'd met a lot of nice people in the years that I'd been a chef, I inevitably ran into those who felt I was inferior solely due to the chromosomes I'd been born with. And I'd watched enough Interstellar Chef shows to know how vicious the competitions could be. The guys made sure the women didn't stand a chance.

This wouldn't just be about cooking. No, my very survival could come into play.

Well, let them behave however they pleased. I'd watch out for threats and when the day was over, I'd be the one smiling.

The hatch opened, and I strutted down the ramp to the ground, still huffing about the injustice of me being the only female competitor.

That's when I realized the only way to make this better was to prove—again, like always—I was worthy.

So reminiscent to my life growing up.

However, I'd been selected for this contest because someone felt I could win, and far be it for me to disprove that theory.

When my feet touched the ground, the rotten egg smell of swamp grass hit my sinuses. Welcome to Trillaphon, the planet that was only a lizard's prime vacation destination. We were expected to prepare meals here?

No, we were expected to punt, to do what we could with the odd ingredients they'd provide.

I could do this. No one could beat my sauces. My delicate hand with a pasta.

My determination to win.

Throm joined me on the ground, his gorgeous light blue eyes sparkling. "Has anyone ever told you they respect your spunk?"

My face heated, but I only cocked one brow in his direction. I knew what he was doing: cozying up to me. Sure, we'd declared a truce, but there was no way we'd ever be friends.

"Welcome," Jell shouted, soaring over the trees to hover in front of us. Camera bots followed his every movement, and his pink skin shone like he'd greased it up with biergart fat.

"The show will commence soon," Jell zipped over to Throm and stroked his arm. "Nice, very nice. Lads and ladies, have you gotten a view of his muscles?" He waved to the closest camera bots. "Take some vids from all angles. The other males too." His frown turned to me. "You are not wearing the skirt left in your cabin."

"Yeah, it ripped when I was tugging it up over my hips," I said. My voice came out completely sincere, but I was sure my eyes gleamed with mischief, so I trained my gaze at the ground as if I were embarrassed. "I'm terribly sorry. They sent the wrong size. I do hope my pants will suffice until I can change into the clothing the show will provide for the event."

Jell huffed, but there wasn't much he could do about it. The skirt had a rip in it—now.

"Very well. Camera bots!" He signaled for them to take vids of us from all angles as we followed him. "If you please, I'll take you to where you can change into your tunics and mentally prepare for the show. The first event takes place in twenty minues, and our glorious audience cannot wait for the show to begin."

The show was recorded; they'd release it in a few lunar cycles, so no one cared but us.

Jell started down a recently cut path through the jungle with us following.

Muggy heat clouded the air, making it a challenge to breathe. My shoes sunk into the boggy soil, and I scooted from side to side to avoid thorny vines snaking out across the path.

Throm remained behind me, and his stare glided down my backside like a heavy caress.

My heart tripped, and not from exerting myself in the sweltering air.

How was I going to finish this show without giving into my urge to devour him?

My mind kept skipping back to how wonderful his mouth felt claiming mine, the heady feeling of his hands on my flesh, and the slick way he'd helped me out of my panties with a lust-filled grin on his face.

We emerged from the path and out into a big clearing. Scissor drones hummed around the outer edges, cutting back encroaching vines, while others worked at tree-top height to suspend an awning over the cooking area set up on the opposite side of the field

Five grills with synthesizers beneath sat beside counters with drawers, I assume the latter holding cooking implements and spices. In most of the multi-verse, people had long since stopped cooking with real ingredients, finding it easier to use synthesizers to prepare a meal in seconds.

The art of combining new flavors and experimenting with spices was shoved to the side by convenience. True cooking was reserved for formal occasions and when someone went out for a fine meal.

Hence the high demand for trained chefs.

"Amazing," Aesoars said from beside me, and we shared a grin. Maybe he wouldn't act snide. "You're going to find this a true challenge, human. It's unlike the rodents you prepared on the space station, correct?"

So much for me thinking he might be nice. "I'm always up for a good challenge. And just so you know, my rat stir fry is known throughout the galaxy."

My gaze caught Throm's, and he nodded, biting back a laugh.

"Why do you keep making flashy eyes at him?" Aesoars asked, shooting a dark look Throm's way. "He's a competitor. Forbidden. He will not help you win. If anything, he'll make sure you lose. Women are always knocked out in the first round."

"Not this woman."

"I will make sure of it."

Gee, thanks for the reminder that he'd look for an opportunity to sabotage me before the end of the event.

"And just so you know, I don't need Throm's favor to win," I added.

There was no harm in being nice to each other, was there? We cooked, we presented our dishes, and the judges decided which was best. Being mean wouldn't add to the points, although I'd heard the audience ate it up.

I sighed and walked around him to stand on the other side of Throm.

Along the back section of the meadow, I spied big chill boxes full of ingredients unlike any I'd seen before. Trillaphon delicacies we'd use during the competition.

The grass beneath my feet had been cut tight to the ground, probably by the scissor drones before we arrived.

Camera bots zipped around us, collecting footage from all angles. I brushed one aside when it got too close to my face, but for the most part, I'd ignore them. Without them, we had no show.

"Your outfits await you in the changing areas," Jell said, flicking his fingers toward a building with five doors sitting on the right side of the clearing.

I started in that direction, turning back when Throm didn't follow.

"You're not changing?" I asked him.

"He should cook with no clothing," Jell suggested with a snicker.

Throm's brow ridge lifted. "What do you think, Wren?"

"Why would anyone compete in the show naked?" I asked, unable to tell if he joked or not.

"Everything's about ratings," Jell chimed in.

I glided my gaze down Throm's front. Many watched the show; it was one of the most popular series throughout the multi-universe. And if flashing his ass and other . . . assets made watchers eager, I could see why they'd tried to talk him into it.

"I still can't believe you'd do something like that." We would be cooking. Heat, sizzling fat, whatever. He could be injured.

"Ah, so you are here for the eye treat. They didn't select you for your skills as a chef," Aesoars said as he sauntered past Throm.

Throm's gaze went steely, and for a second, I saw the generations of warriors from his past in the ridges rippling down from his neck to the way his thick tail whipped behind him. "Never doubt my skills as a chef, Aesoars. Never."

Despite there being many universes in the interstellar federation, the world was small. People talked and scorning someone who might win the show and cater a meal fit for royalty could be a big mistake. Aesoars could soon find himself synthing foogar strips in a back alley McDiners.

Aesoars backed up a pace. "I, uh . . . I need to go change." He darted toward the hut and opened the first door on the left, scooting inside. It banged shut behind him.

"Good luck today," Throm told me, his voice pretty

much cooling the air around me. "And yes, I *am* going to change into a tunic and pants. If they want someone to put on a strip tease, they'll have to hit up Omyn."

"Thank you." I leaned close and dropped my voice so the camera bots wouldn't pick up what I said. "I didn't believe for a secunda that you'd compete naked."

"No, but you would've looked, right?" he asked softly. "Were you hoping I'd say yes and give you a good view of my assets, Wren?"

Heat baked my face. Damn, did this guy fluster me.

I could give it back as well as I could take it. "Maybe I was."

6

THROM

My species were known for their strong sexual appetites, especially with their fated mates. I'd craved this female from the moment I spied her sitting with her friends on the other side of the bar. After taking the com call and arranging for my sister to be transported to the best medical facility possible, I'd darted back into the bar, looking for Wren. Not finding her had almost ripped me apart.

I hadn't wanted to be with anyone else since.

Would it help if I mentioned that fact to her?

I'd growl in frustration if it didn't draw the camera bots' attention. This wasn't the right time. But soon, the competition would be over. I'd play it safe and hold myself back, but I would not leave her this time. I'd show her all of me, and if that didn't convince her I was worthy of her, I would let her slip away.

"Maybe I'll give you a private showing one of these days," I said as we strode toward the changing rooms. "We have breaks. The camera bots won't be with us all the time."

"It's forbidden," she hissed. Her cheeks went pink at my words, something I'd read was common with humans when they were either embarrassed or sexually excited. I fully intended to see her blushing like this due to the latter one day soon.

"It would be naughty," she added, shaking her finger my way.

I couldn't help myself.

"Maybe I enjoy being naughty," I said, playing her game. "But I imagine looking is all right. Touching might take things into uneasy territory." *Uneasy* being an understatement. I'd burst into flames if she touched.

We played a game that could get both of us in trouble.

She had a goal here, as did I, and both of us couldn't win the final prize.

Besides, we'd be kicked off the show if we gave in to our needs.

7
WREN

I caught Jell's narrowed gaze pointed our way. If he hadn't been preening for the camera bots, I had a feeling he'd zip in front of us and ask us what was going on between us.

"I'm going to get changed," I said breezily, as if Throm was just an acquaintance. It was time to run away rather than flirt.

How had I gone from keeping him at arm's length to wanting to drag him closer? I'd be stupid to endanger everything I came here to win. The creature shelter was in desperate need of funds. This was my chance to truly make a difference.

And without credits, I couldn't fully put my past behind me.

Throm noticed Jell watching. "I'll see you later, then." He strode to one of the doors and stepped inside.

I scooted into the remaining empty room, realizing I was the only one left to change when I passed the three other guys dressed in starched tunics with the show's logo, plus white pants.

"We're watching you," Omyn snarled.

"Creepy dudes do things like that," I shot back, but my hand trembled as I locked the door behind me. It was easy to sink back into the mood I'd found with Throm on Quazar 3. He was funny, a great dancer, and a hotter-than-anything kisser.

I needed to remember I was here for a cooking contest. He was my strongest competition. Only one person would win, and since that had to be me, it was time to be cutthroat.

I could be crafty with whatever I plated.

Blowing the cooking world away was my goal.

After changing my clothes, I yanked my hair up high and secured it snugly with a band, making sure no stray wisps would drift into my face during an important moment.

This wasn't a beauty pageant, so there was no one running around doing our hair or make-up. Jell? Probably, but he was the host. In fact, we'd been told to make sure we looked natural, that the surveyed audience preferred seeing contestants who represented the average person from their planet.

That was me. A regular old Earth girl.

I emerged as the camera bots were converging on where the others waited for the show to begin. Tiny lights flashed on the top of the bots' round shells, telling me countdown mode had begun.

A spike of nervousness jolted through me, making my hands shake. I sucked in a breath and released it. Did it again. Over and over until calm nudged aside my panic. I could do this. I had the ability to succeed inside me. I was so much more than the life I grew up in.

Great words to repeat in my head.

My gaze sought Throm's, but he was chatting with Jell. He didn't look my way, and he gave no indication he cared if I was present or not.

Good. That was how it should be.

The camera bots started humming and Jell left Throm to take his place in front of a bank of blazing lights.

Someone darted in and smoothed his wedged hair, though it looked amazing already. Another alien blotted his face to reduce the sheen.

It was hot already, and I hadn't even stepped into the kitchen.

A voice called out from overhead. "Attention. Ten secunda. Nine . . . Eight . . ."

Jell waved for us to approach and stand on one of the five X's painted on the ground in front of him. We filed over to that area and lined up. This put me shoulder to . . . well, lower arm, with Throm.

"When we rush to the mini kitchens, pick a spot on one of *my* sides," he whispered as the countdown continued.

"You're not planning any tricks, are you?" I said it completely in jest. If nothing else, I didn't doubt this guy's integrity, not after he'd explained what happened on Quazar 3. If anything, I was finding it hard not to let my admiration turn into affection—a dangerous emotion right there. Affection for Throm was only a step away from love.

Damn, I wasn't allowing my feelings to drift in that direction.

"We have a truce." He flashed his tusks. "I won't sabotage you, and you won't attack me. This way, we won't have to guard both sides."

"You're right. We have a truce, but . . ."

He nodded as the voice called out three. Two freakin' secunda left before showtime!

"And roll 'em," the announcer said.

"Welcome back, everyone," Jell cried. "As you can see, our competitors have gotten serious. No more frolicking about without clothing. It's time for this season's Interstellar Chef!"

"But what?" Throm asked as Jell introduced Omyn, who raced over to Jell, doing a backflip through the air on the way. He paused, jogging in place, while the crew reran his interview from last night for the viewers who missed it. Omyn's recorded voice echoed in the small meadow.

"Throm Nargoth," Jell cried, waving for him to approach.

"But what?" he asked me patiently.

Like, the audience would wait for me to finish?

"Wren?" he prompted.

I gave him a steely look. "I won't attack you but be aware that you're fair game if it comes down to just me and you."

8

THROM

That was fair. If we could make it to the final round, there was nothing that would stop me from doing all I could to win. However, I drew the line at hurting or sabotaging her. The viewers might groan, and their pretend messages would flash in the sky, demanding I knock her from the round before it was finished, but I wouldn't do it.

This wasn't only about getting into her panties again. I wanted more.

The matebond symbol on my right inner wrist flared whenever I was near her. Nothing and no one would keep me from claiming her now that I'd found her again. Which was a problem with the contest, but I'd find a way through it.

One of us would win, but it would be the person who prepared the best dish, not the one who ducked when a chopping block went flying through the air.

Jell introduced each of us. When he'd finished, he flashed his tusks toward the camera bots. "And with that, I think it's time to get the show started, don't you?" He drew out the silence like a maestro at an award-winning performance. So long that the fake audience piped in from somewhere above groaned. "Chefs, choose your stations!"

We whirled around and raced toward the grills. I kept an eye on Wren, pleased when she took a spot on the end where she'd have no one on her left. I shouldered Omyn out of the way and claimed the one on her right.

She flashed me a subtle smile, reaching up to scratch her nose to hide it. Her nod after confirmed her thanks.

Jell zipped above us, the camera bots following like eager pluffas. The pups clung so close to their mother, they often tripped her. "I imagine you're all excited to see our mystery ingredient, aren't you?"

The fake audience shrieked in excitement.

"But before I deliver it to you," Jell said. "I want to ensure you understand the rules." Tipping his head back, he released his famous cackle. "Actually, there are no rules except no foochie-moochie-feelies among you. If you're caught in a, shall we say, compromising position, you will be kicked off the show and sent home in shame."

My gaze met Wren's, and she dragged hers away, focusing on Jell.

Jell floated sideways in front of us. "Other than that, you have twenty minues to plate a dish for our exclusive judges. Prepare something that will knock their feet off," he pouted, "not really. But impress them with your culinary expertise, my illustrious chefs. You must use the mystery ingredient and at least three local items you'll find in our vast chillers." One of his limbs swept toward them standing behind us. "And, other than that . . ." Drums beat in a rapidly increasing rhythm from somewhere overhead. "Anything. Else. Goes!"

Omyn, who had taken the station to my right, rubbed his hands together, his two heads bobbing into each other.

The eyes of one spun toward the other competitors, while the head on my side turned to watch me intently.

"Anything goes, anything goes," Aesoars cried, dancing in a circle with his limbs lifted.

Crik'ee giggled with glee and rocked on his heels. They'd claimed the stations beyond Omyn.

"Without further ado . . ." Jell shouted. "I present the mystery ingredient for the appetizer round, live scoldarns!"

Scoldarn. Scoldarn. I tried to remember—

Something smacked into my shoulders and clung. While I twisted and wrenched it off my spine, another plopped onto the grill in front of Wren.

She grabbed a knife off the counter block and with a whack, severed the multi-limbed creature's spine.

I flipped mine onto the butcher block to the right of my grill and did the same, ending the writhing, hissing plant's life. Ah, yes, scoldarns grew in the jungles of Trillaphon. They were said to taste like scallops, though they came from the vegetable family.

A strangled cry from my right was cut off. I spun to find a scoldarn fusing itself to Aesoars's face. He staggered around, tripping over his limbs.

Wren raced past me with a knife lifted in her hand. She leapt on top of Aesoars, bringing him to the ground. He whimpered; his guttural shrieks cut off by the scoldarn digging into his face.

She delicately sliced along the back of the scoldarn while I rushed over to help, cutting deeply with my own blade. She reached the plant's spine first and severed it. The scoldarn went limp.

She settled on her heels and glanced up at me, her eyes wide with dismay.

The scoldarn wasn't moving but neither was Aesoars.

"We have a scoldarn issue," Jell cried with excitement. "I wonder what will happen next. As I said, anything goes during Interstellar Chef! Will the Brevulian discover not everyone is as peaceful as his race or . . ." He looked up at the sky as if the viewers were there, but only the camera bots hovered nearby. "Or will we eliminate one competitor this easily?"

Wren shook her head and pried one of the scoldarn's limbs off Aesoars's face, followed by more, each sticking as much as the last. Finally, with all the limbs curving upward, she lifted the main body off Aesoars's face. A sucking sound echoed around us as it released. Wren tossed the scoldarn toward the chillers.

She placed her finger on Aesoars' neck, checking for a pulse, then shrugged. "I can't tell." Her voice lifted. "How do I tell?"

"Seventeen minues," Jell cried. "Seventeen minues left to plate your dishes!"

Fuck the dishes. I dropped down beside Aesoars and shook his shoulder. "Wake up."

Drones flew from the woods, their mechanical arms extended. They shoved me and Wren out of the way and latched onto Aesoars's limbs.

"I'm afraid one contestant will not receive a high score for this round," Jell said solemnly. "But this is Interstellar Chef, where anything goes!"

Crik'ee shrieked in dismay as the drones lifted Aesoars and whisked him into the jungle.

9
WREN

"Fifteen freakin' minues," I snarled, grabbing Throm's arm as I raced past him to reach my station. I ditched him at his own and ran to the chillers, trying to decide what I'd make as I poured over the items up for grabs.

Omyn was busily chopping a bunch of green things, and for all I knew, they were meat and not vegetables. He'd claimed his plates and already had a bright orange sauce swirled across the white plexi surface.

From what I'd read, though I'd never prepared them, scoldarns were quite tasty if cooked to the point where they started to soften. Slightly sweet, they had a spiciness many found appealing. So, sweet and spicy appetizer.

Ah, ha. I had an idea. I just needed . . .

I moved along the chillers, staring through the clear plex, before grabbing three items out of the last upright box in the row. I scurried back to my station, snagging plates from the general supply counter as I passed. After placing everything on my butcher block, I got to work, first pulling out a pan to sauté the scoldarn, setting it on the heat conductor and turning the burner to a medium-low setting.

When the pan was hot, I plopped in a blob of biergart fat, the latest craze. The rendered oil had a nice, nutty flavor that would pair wonderfully with the scoldarn.

It didn't take long to peel back the scoldarn's skin, revealing the pale purple flesh beneath. I tossed aside the main body, not having time to debone it, and focused on two of the larger limbs, cleaning them quickly and slicing them into thin, completely round pieces. They soon sizzled in the pan, and I got to work on my three other ingredients. One, I left raw, though I added a few slices to give them an artistic appeal. The other two items went into the blaster, and after applying bursts, they soon formed a creamy sauce. I added pinches of select spices and gave the sauce another whirl.

"Five minues, people," Jell said. "Five minues left. Make sure your plates are prepared!"

While I was still determined to craft the best dish I could and win whatever prize would be awarded at the end of this event, I no longer had to worry about losing and being booted off the show. With Aesoars out of the equation, all of us were safe today.

"One minue," Jell cried. "One minue. Oh, I am so excited to see what you've all prepared. Who will win the first round of Interstellar Chef?"

While camera bots caught my movements from all angles, I lightly poked the scoldarn and found it exactly the rubbery texture I was aiming for. After drizzling my sauce across the plate in delicate swirls, I carefully placed the scoldarn slices on it, laying them a way that would appear tasty as well as attractive. I strategically splashed sauce on top of them, then laid the final ingredient among the slices. The mix of colors made the dish pop.

"*And . . .* Your time is up," Jell called out.

With a grunt, I stepped away from my station, noting how gorgeous Throm's plates appeared.

My shoulders drooped when I saw Omyn and Crik'ee's plates looked equally fantastic. The competition was going to be stiff. I'd done my best, and it was too late to add anything to my dishes to make them stand out a bit more.

"Our judges are ready," Jell said, soaring past our stations, commenting on each of our dishes. "Lovely presentation and oh, I love what you did with the scoldarn," he said about mine.

After speaking to each of us, he did a backflip away from us and zoomed close to the camera bots. "Hover beams? It's time to do your jobs!"

I stepped away from my plates as beams of light shot down from the sky, focused on our offerings. Our plates shot up through the beams to the judges waiting in an exclusive dining room on a spaceship orbiting the planet. The judges wouldn't come down to where we cooked.

No way.

They were so elite; they rode on golden whizzers and never placed their feet on the ground.

We waited in silence while the camera bots zoomed in on each of us to capture any excitement, angst, or fear lingering on our faces.

Cries of "*Oh!*" and "*Ah!*" were piped down to us from the judges, but we had no way of knowing which dishes they enjoyed the most until—

"Lovely contestants," Jell bellowed. "We have . . . Oh, my gosh." He slapped his palms against his cheeks. "I cannot believe it. It's wonderful. Stupendous. Amazing!" He rubbed his many limbs together, and the spikes on his shoulders quivered. "It appears we have . . ."

A drumroll echoed in the small clearing.

Jell soared toward us. "Chefs, we have a tie. A tie, I say. Something very rare on Interstellar Chef."

Ah . . . I swallowed; my throat felt dryer than the Prooleer Desert.

Tension made my hands twitch and my spine quiver. Maybe I should've added more lardine to my sauce? What if I'd cooked the scoldarn too long or not enough? The dish had to be prepared perfectly or it got too rubbery. I worried the final ingredient I'd included had been too crispy when compared to the soft, gelatinous scoldarn.

I bit back my snarl and kept my face neutral. No reason to hand the viewers my anxiety to savor like their favorite dish.

"The winners of the appetizer round are . . ." Jell grinned, revealing his fangs he'd had encrusted with jewels. His ancestors could rip off a troolon's leg with one bite of their fangs, which was saying something, since troolons were about fifteen feet tall. Jell wasn't going to be biting anything but perfectly cooked scoldarn.

"Hurry," Omyn yelled, his face bright with fury. "We wait too long."

Crik'ee cackled and shuffled his feet. "Impatient, Omyn?"

Jell zipped over to hover in front of them. "The winners of this round are Crik'ee and Omyn!"

Damn. My gut sunk. I'd lost the first round.

Crik'ee leaped around, his arms in the air. Omyn scowled.

"However," Jell said softly. I could picture our entire future audience leaning forward, some oozing through their wade pools, toward view screens, others sitting forward on their cushions, desperate to hear what might happen next.

The end of a round was not always the end of the game.

"Only one of you may claim the prize," Jell finished, waving his limbs in big circles.

"It mine. It mine!" Omyn shrieked.

"I believe you two will have to decide who claims it," Jell said blandly, studying his claws.

The camera bots encircled the two males.

Crik'ee stumbled away from Omyn. His frantic gaze raked the jungle, seeking escape.

Omyn stalked him, his six arms lifted, the single, thick claws extended.

They circled each other, Crik'ee pleading, Omyn snarling, spittle flying from his mouth.

Omyn leaped onto Crik'ee, knocking him onto his back. He ripped into Crik'ee's right arm with his fangs and claws.

While I gaped in horror, Omyn severed Crik'ee's right arm.

He leapt up and off the platform, dancing around the meadow with Crik'ee's arm lifted and a wild look in his eyes. "I wins. I wins!"

10

THROM

Crik'ee sat up and snarled at Omyn. Green blood squirted from his shoulder as he scrambled to his feet. He scowled down at where his arm used to be and the blood spurts slowed, the wound sealing off. His species healed quickly; they were incredibly difficult to kill. Hence the females of their species coming into heat only every ten seasons. If they could breed more often, their planet would be overrun.

"Whoa," Wren said from my side, gaping at Crik'ee.

"Watch," I whispered, grinning at the amazement blazing across her face.

In no time, a new limb sprouted from Crik'ee's shoulder.

When he staggered, drones soared over to him and lifted him. They swept him up, over the jungle, aiming for where we'd left the shuttle.

"His arm will be fully formed by morning," I said. "Losing the fight will cost him the prize, but it won't hold him back during the event tomorrow. He'll be tired and need to sleep, but Omyn will be too busy with whatever prize he wins to take advantage of Crik'ee when he's unconscious. And we'll leave him alone to heal."

"Why would anyone sneak into his room and hurt him?" she asked in wide-eyed dismay.

"To keep him from being able to compete in the next event. If he didn't show up, he'd automatically lose." I couldn't help myself, though I kept my voice low. Thankfully, the camera bots remained hyper focused on Crik'ee. "Would you be willing to sneak into my room and tackle me? We can wrestle. I promise I won't . . . hurt you."

Her laugh shot out, and her shoulders loosened, the exact thing I was aiming for. To survive this event, she'd need to remain alert. Tension wore a person out. She'd be exhausted by the time we reached the final event if she didn't relax.

"And that's the end of today's show," Jell yelled. He waved to Omyn. "Our viewers have cooked up a special surprise for you—an evening in the loosh pool on this very planet." He launched into advertising mode, telling us who'd sponsored the gift. "The Veesar Corporation liaison will meet you when your shuttle lands and escort you to the pool. The evening comes complete with meals prepared by elite, Veesar chefs and a bottle of whichever leekar you prefer. Again, we can thank Veesar Corporation for generously donating your prize."

Omyn's jaw dropped. "Loosh pool?"

Jell grinned, the jewels on his fangs flashing in the light. "Yes, isn't it amazing? Please remain behind while the chefs depart in the shuttle." He stared at a primary camera bot. "And that's it for this event, lovely viewers. Join us again soon for the next episode of . . . Interstellar Chef!"

The lights went out on the top of the camera bots, and Jell's face smoothed. He soared over to Omyn. "Lovely touch in the end, my friend. Ripping off his arm is truly inspired. Our audience will be thrilled when the show releases."

Omyn grinned, revealing his three rows of upper and lower jagged teeth. "Shoulda rip leg off too."

"I do love how you think." Jell's gaze swept over us, but now that the cameras were no longer recording, it was clear he'd dismissed us from his mind. We'd be back on center stage again for the next event, but for now, we were of no more use to him than the drones bustling around, cleaning up the equipment.

Wren scooted over to stand near me, keeping her voice down. "I know leekar can make you silly if you drink too much, but what's a loosh pool?"

Omyn glared our way, though he had no reason to attack.

Wren gulped and stepped close enough to me that the warmth of her skin made my skin tingle.

"A loosh pool is huge. It's full of a special emollient that softens the skin. I've heard it can even be orgasmic if you lounge in one long enough."

She gaped up at me. "Really?"

"Really." I wiggled my brow ridge. "If we'd shared a tied win, I wouldn't have ripped off your arm."

Her lips curled upward before smoothing. "That's a relief."

"There is one thing I would've done if I'd won, however." I jumped off the platform, and she followed.

We strode into the jungle, taking the path that would return us to the shuttle. Jell stuffed a life support helmet on his head and engaged his hover jets. He soared through the clouds, heading for his ship orbiting the planet. He'd meet us at our next destination.

Wren caught up and trotted beside me. "What's the one thing you would've done if you'd won?"

"I would've made sure you were in that pool beside me and . . ."

She stopped on the trail, her fingers fluttering at her sides. "And what?"

I glanced around to ensure we were alone before speaking near her ear. Because she was so utterly tempting, and I had no way of resisting her lure, I took my time before speaking, gliding my lips along her jawline to her ear. Her skin quivered, but she didn't pull away.

She placed her palm on my chest, and her smoldering gaze met mine.

Just like at the bar, we couldn't keep our hands off each other. This contest was going to be sweet torture.

"And what, Throm?" she said, her voice thready.

"The orgasms you'd receive would've come from me, not the emollient."

11
WREN

My blood had started singing Throm's song.

I backed away from him, bringing the music to a screeching halt.

I wanted to snarl at him for heating me up like that. It wasn't fair. We weren't allowed to hook up even if I wanted to make it happen. And I didn't.

Growling, I stormed past him, stomping up the trail toward the ship that would take us back to the shuttle.

He stepped in behind me, covering my back. I expected him to touch me or tease me some more, but his eyes remained alert, and he kept scanning the jungle around us.

To distract myself from everything Throm, I focused on the show, unable to believe what just happened to Crik'ee. I knew this contest could be deadly. Hello. The prize was a shipload of money. But still, I'd never been convinced the "deaths" I witnessed weren't being faked.

Now I'd seen one contestant rip off another's arm. I'd seen our mystery food item smother another, and we still didn't know what happened to him.

This shit was real, and if I wasn't careful, something like

that could happen to me, especially if I wasn't paying attention.

"You're too much of a distraction," I snarled at Throm over my shoulder.

"So are you."

"We need to agree we won't do anything until this is over."

"I'll try," he said.

"If you can hold yourself back, I can too."

His brow ridge rose as one. "Are you sure about that?"

I huffed and rolled my eyes, then whirled around and stomped along the trail. I didn't want to answer. Just looking at him made me want to stroke his face.

Rip off his pants.

"Do you think Aesoars survived?" I asked, again aiming for distraction. My body ached with a need I couldn't invite Throm to satisfy, but that didn't mean reality wasn't setting in, making me shake with reaction.

"I'm sure he did," Throm said. "It's rare for anyone to die from a scoldarn attachment."

"They won't give us scoldarn again, and whatever they send for the next event could be worse."

"Or better. Let's think positively about this. During the next round, either Crik'ee or Omyn will be eliminated."

Nice that he thought I stood a chance. "If Omyn wins, he'll attack me. Knock me out of the competition instead of outcooking me. I can't grow back a new arm."

"No worries. They'll send drones to help you, and I assume if they can't reattach your arm, they'll give you a cyborg one."

"You're not making me feel better, Throm," I growled. Through the vegetation ahead, I spied the shuttle waiting in the clearing.

He chuckled, but his voice dropped to a low, husky volume that smoothed down my spine. "I won't let him near you."

While it was a thrill that he was confident he could protect me, that wasn't the point.

"Truly," he said, his face deadly serious. "There's no way I'll let anyone harm you. Trust me in this."

He wasn't a warrior. As far as I knew, he was only a chef. And this was Omyn, an alien with six vicious claws and three rows of jagged teeth. On top of that, he sported a mean attitude.

The thing though? I did trust Throm not to cause me physical pain, but what about my heart?

It would be too easy to succumb to his overwhelming charm, to hop into his bed and take my full weight of pleasure, then see him ditch me in the morning. This wasn't me applying his past behavior to our present. He had a valid reason to leave me waiting in that closet. I'd forgiven him.

Nope, I worried he'd see this as a fun way to pass the time while I'd be falling too hard and too fast.

We emerged from the path and continued toward the shuttle, where we were greeted by the pilot.

"We've got a problem," she said.

"In what way?" Throm scratched the back of his neck, shooting me a concerned glance.

Crik'ee sauntered around from behind the ship. His skin lacked color, but he looked a lot better already.

The pilot shifted her hooves on the boggy soil. "The ship's out of commission."

"Tell the show to send another," Throm said. "We need to arrive at the next location before tomorrow."

"I called, and a shuttle's on the way, but . . ." She shrugged. "They'll delay filming the show until we can arrive. That's not the issue. But the new shuttle, a day-trip cruiser sent by the prince himself, will not arrive until morning." Her gaze scanned the jungle.

The sun had sunk below the dense vegetation, and around us, the jungle had started to come alive. Chirps and muted shrieks echoed around us. I hadn't cared when we walked because I had Throm with me, and we'd soon board the ship.

"We'll wait inside until morning," Throm said, urging me past the pilot with his fingers snug on my elbow.

"You can't," the pilot said, turning. "The problem's a gas leak. All the cabins are flooded. If you go inside, you'll succumb to the fumes within minues."

12

THROM

"We'll find shelter here for the night," I said, scanning the jungle.

"We have to stay here, here?" Crik'ee said, his brow hairs lifting. "Things here will eat us." He shivered and turned in circles, peering at the dense vegetation surrounding us. "We need to go back to the meadow where we competed. The drones will help us."

"Good idea." The pilot pulled a gun from the holster on her belt. "Do not worry. I will protect you while we walk to the meadow." She waved the laser pistol around.

Crik'ee yelped. Wren ducked.

I directed the pilot's hand downward. "Watch where you point that, please."

"Oh, sorry." She squinted past the ship, and her solitary purple eye widened.

I turned to find vines snaking across the ground toward us.

"We can't stay here," I barked.

The pilot backed up, and before I could hold her back,

she bolted into the jungle in the direction the three of us had just come from.

"Wait. Wait!" Crik'ee took off after her, his regular length and stubby arms spiraling. "We must run to the meadow. The crew will protect us!"

"Come back," Wren cried. She turned to me. "We need to go after them."

"We do, but . . ." I lifted her off her feet and raced toward the shuttle. A jump, and I landed on the top.

The vines snaked beneath the silver ship, seemingly unaware we stood above them.

"What are th—"

I placed my finger over her mouth, stopping her words, and shook my head.

"Oh," she mouthed, cringing as she peered down at the vines snapping out from the mother plant behind hovering on the edge of the jungle. Some broke off and slunk into the dense vegetation.

I'd read about snisk vines and how the acid they secreted could melt the meat from bones within minues. These newly "birthed" young of the enormous plant would track down prey and bring it back to their mother. The only saving grace was they remained on the ground and didn't slither up trees.

Since they ignored the ship, they must be able to tell it was an inanimate object—not food.

Once the young vines had left the small open area, and the mother had slunk back into the jungle, I relaxed. I sat and tugged Wren down beside me.

She leaned against my side. "What were those things, and are they going to catch Crik'ee and the pilot?"

I explained about the vines and how they hunted.

"Awesome," she said softly, probably as fearful as me

that another mother might hear her speaking. "Poor Crik'ee and the pilot."

I stood. "I'll find and take them someplace safe, then come back for you."

She rose to her feet, her brow wedging together. "I'm going with you."

"You're safer here."

"I'm safer with you." Her arms snaked around her waist, and she peered into the jungle. The sun would soon sink from view, and shrieks of creatures in the jungle had grown louder as night predators began hunting. "We don't know what will come after us next."

While she was right, I felt better knowing she was off the ground then trotting behind me along the path. "I have to move fast."

"I'll keep up."

I watched her face, looking for softening of her resolve, but found only determination.

"All right." I glared at the brilliantly white tunic I'd been provided by the show. "I wish I was wearing something other than this stupid outfit."

"Hey, at least you're not naked. Imagine running through the woods with your junk hanging out."

Junk? My laugh burst out. "You have a point."

She swatted at a bug trying to nibble on her neck.

"Ready?" I asked.

"Sure. Is there any place safe on this planet?"

"If there is, I'll find it."

"We could go to wherever they took Omyn," she said. "He wouldn't be staying here for the night if it wasn't in a safe location."

"From what I understand, the pool isn't near this location. He was transported to the mountains and flown deep inside a dormant volcano."

"That's too far a walk."

"In this jungle? Yes." I lifted her into my arms and with a leap, returned us to the ground.

"Nice trick," she said. "I can barely jump over a log."

I took her hand. "We're going to run now, Wren."

Biting her lip, she nodded.

I bolted for the path with her racing behind me.

Halfway to the meadow, we heard calls from above us. We came to a stop and looked up, spying Crik'ee and the pilot perching on a branch far from the ground. They clung to each other.

"Don't bother going to the meadow," Crik'ee said. "They're gone!" His low, mournful cry rang out. "Only drones remained, and they ignored us. I thought of jumping on one and getting ride, but I can't breathe in outer space without a life support helmet."

Neither could we.

"Move over," I said softly, not wanting to draw the attention of the vines that appeared—so far—to have left the area.

"There's no room," Crik'ee hissed, waving to the narrow bit of branch remaining. "Find your own tree."

"You can't stay there all night."

Crik'ee glared. "Oh yes, we can."

I sighed. If I forced this, of course we could squish onto the branch beside them. But it would be a tight fit. A quick glance around didn't show any other decent sized trees in the area, and I wasn't sure we'd be safe even off the ground, though I'd chance it.

"Are you ready to run some more?" I asked Wren.

"Yup. Where will we go?"

"We'll find our own tree, as Crik'ee has so kindly suggested." I was determined to find a safe place to wait for morning.

Wren's ragged breathing made me wish we could take time to rest, but we couldn't.

She gave me a brave nod. "Lead on."

"Return to the ship in the morning," the pilot called down. "We will wait for you, but . . ."

She didn't need to finish the sentence.

If we didn't appear by a certain time, they'd assume something had killed us.

13
WREN

"I didn't think a cooking show would involve running," I panted as I jogged through the jungle with Throm.

"You haven't seen anything yet. One season, the contestants literally had to cook while scaling a mountain."

Of course, he wasn't short of breath. My lungs raged like I was only halfway through a triathlon.

"Do you . . . work out?" I panted.

He shot me a smile. "Sure, don't you?"

Not enough.

"How . . . did the contestants cook . . . while . . . scaling a mountain?" When this was over, I was going to make time to get more exercise. Cooking produced wonderful, yummy food, and I ate too much of it.

"Floating cooking stations remained with them. They carried their chosen ingredients in pouches and prepared them on the hovering stone surface. Plates appeared beside them at their command."

At least I'd missed out on participating in that season.

I looked around, hoping I'd spy a tree we could climb. *He* could climb, that is. My upper body strength wasn't any better than my lung capacity. If I were alone, I'd find a hole in the ground or dig beneath some bushes—where, sadly, the vines would find me.

"There it is," he said, tugging me off a thin, animal trail and to the right. He stopped at the base of a big tree and peered up, pointing. "If we can reach that branch, we can stay there until morning."

Ah, the joys of camping in the woods. Jungle. Whatever.

A crack rang out behind me, and I scooted forward, grabbing onto Throm's back. Clinging.

"I can't get up there alone," I said softly, peering around but seeing nothing.

"Climb on, and I'll take you up there with me."

"My arms around your neck will choke you."

He peered at me over his shoulder. "Then hold onto my shoulders."

"Okay." I bit down hard on my lower lip. He'd do the hard work, but it wasn't going to be easy holding on.

I jumped and latched onto his shoulders, taking care not to scrape my hand on the sharp points on the ends of his coiling horns. I slid my legs around his waist.

"Ready?" he asked.

"As I'll ever be."

Something tickled down my back, but I wasn't looking. "We need to leave. Now."

He leapt upward, and something slid down my back as he moved, scrambling to grab onto my ass on the way by. Throm left it behind, soaring upward.

"Nice thigh muscles," I said inanely, as he grabbed onto a low branch that was too small and close to the ground to be safe for the night. I didn't know much about trees, but ten feet or so was not going to be far enough away from killer vines.

"Thanks," he said with a low laugh. He wrangled us up until he could stand on the slender branch. "I'm going to use those thigh muscles again." A chuckle came through in his words.

"Go for it."

Another jump took us higher, then a third. He kept climbing and leaping until he'd taken us a dizzying height from the ground.

"This should do," he said, casually bracing his palm against the tree trunk.

"Can the vines reach all the way up here?" I slid off his back, and holding onto the back of his shirt, peered down, watching as vines scrambled across the forest floor, deprived of a meal of us so far.

"I don't think so."

I wasn't sure why they couldn't, but sometimes, it made my heart race less when I didn't think too hard about something. If they started climbing, we'd worry then.

Throm settled on the wide branch with his back to the trunk. His legs splayed around the sides, and he patted the spot in front of him. "Sit."

I dropped down, presenting my butt in his direction. It felt too intimate to straddle him, though my body suggested it might be fun. Bad body.

His arms went around me, though loosely, and I was confident he wouldn't let me fall.

The sun fully set, and like someone shut off the lights, the world around us went dark. Creatures scurried along the forest floor, and cries and howls echoed across distant treetops.

I swallowed, convinced I wasn't going to sleep a wink.

"Here we are," I finally said.

"And here we will remain until morning."

"Someone for the show will look for us, right?" The complete confidence I'd arrived here with had fled. What if we ended up stranded here forever? We had no food or water and—

His arms tightened around me, and he rested his chin on my shoulder, taking care not to scrape my face with his horn. "They will come if for nothing other than the fact that the show will demand it."

That wasn't reassuring.

"They had no problem letting the scoldarn attack Aesoars," I said.

"Because that was part of the show. Besides, scoldarns are rarely deadly."

"The 'rarely' in your statement is what worries me most." I placed my hands on his forearms. "I know you'll do all you can to protect me."

"You are right."

To think I'd cursed this guy for a month or more after he bailed on me back on Quasar 3. A few hours together shouldn't have been enough to form a connection, but we had.

"What's going to protect you? I don't have a knife and didn't think to grab a stick or rock before you scaled the tree."

"I can defend us both."

"Do you know self-defense moves? I almost took a course once." But I decided I couldn't spare the credits when it came down to food or classes.

My tiny bedroom door would rattle too many times when I was growing up. I'd lie underneath my bed, praying the lock would hold. But I was hungry too.

"I've had a lot of training, and self-defense is just a small part of it," he said.

"When?"

"Do you have time for a story?"

I laughed, and while my voice started out tight, it loosened. Maybe there was something to everyone saying humor could relax a person. It released endorphins or something like that.

"I can give you an hour or so," I said, smiling.

"What will you do with the winnings?"

"You assume I'm going to win? That's sweet of you."

His chest moved with his low laugh. "Maybe I'm humoring you."

I poked his thigh. It truly was a nice thigh. Thick and muscular, and it had helped carry us to the top of a tree where we'd be safe. "Time to spill my heart out?"

"Only if you want to. You can tell me to go fuck myself if you prefer."

"I don't mind sharing. What I want most is to win the catering job. I lost my chef's position on the space station, but that's not the only reason. I've pretty much raised myself. My mom? Well, let's just say she enjoyed life."

"It's good to savor every moment, but I can tell by your voice you don't mean she laughed and hugged others a lot."

"Can you call inviting a different guy into our tiny apartment over night after night giving lots of hugs?" I huffed. "I'm not shaming her. She enjoyed sex, and she had it a lot. No harm in that. But sometimes, the guys she brought back were mean."

"To both of you."

My heart sunk, and my voice dropped off to almost nothing. "Yeah."

"I'm sorry."

"She had a bad rep on the space station, but it wasn't

because she liked lots of sex. She didn't like working, always saying it was easier to just take what she needed."

"And you grew up watching all that."

"It haunts me still. By the time I was fourteen, I was determined to make a better life for myself. And when she took off when I was sixteen, I used that as my chance to start over. But no one was willing to believe that my mom's daughter would be any better than her." I hadn't shared this with anyone. I had friends—who didn't? —but if they hadn't heard about my past, I didn't dump it all over them. "I'm sorry."

"Why?"

"It's shameful to talk about stuff like this."

"You were a kid. The shame is that your mother didn't parent you like she should've."

"You're right. Anyway." I sucked in a breath and sent my sadness out of my lungs with the air. "I learned everything about cooking by working my way up, starting first in a sleezy diner on the space station. But they gave me the job, and I worked hard at it, taking tips from the others in the kitchen. Eventually, I took better jobs in nicer places, though I remained on the space station. Winning Interstellar Chef will give me my dream job. Imagine preparing the meal for a prince's wedding reception. No one will look down on me after that."

"I see you as a brave, strong woman."

"I *had* to be. I didn't necessarily *want* to be brave and strong. But if I didn't try, I knew I'd slip into the patterns my mother taught me. I didn't want that for myself. I'm better than that. I'm not her."

He hugged me, and his breath skated across my ear, soothing me. "You're amazing."

My heart lightened at his words. "Thank you."

"How did we end up meeting on Quazar 3?"

"I was a chef on a cruise ship. I did that for a few years, but I didn't like that I had no solid place to call home. They bunked a bunch of us together, and you basically can only claim your bunk as your own. I quit not long after we met and returned to the station."

"Returning to what was familiar."

"There's comfort in that, even if we know we might slip back into the old situation."

"The catering job is a permanent way out of that life."

"That about sums it up, but . . . It's more than that. It's a way of earning respect. I was always the kid people accused of stealing, the one who, if there was trouble going on, I had to be involved. It didn't matter if I wasn't near the place when it happened. My mom handed me her bad rep, and no one believed me."

"That's not fair."

"It wasn't, but it's the life I lived thanks to my mom. They said I was just like her, a whore and a thief. But she was more complex than that. I think she really did love me at one time. She did things she shouldn't have sometimes, but she'd always tell me she'd made a mistake, that she'd try harder. I believe she kept trying until the day she took off."

"Did you suspect foul play?"

"She left a note saying I was old enough to take care of myself now, that she and Frizar—the guy she'd slept with the night before—were going to take a ship and go see the stars. I didn't hear from her after that, so I guess she was right. I *was* old enough to take care of myself."

"I don't know what to say except I'm sorry and that I admire you a lot. I respect you a lot." His arms tightened around me.

"If I win, the money will help me start a new life. Is it bad that I want to escape?"

"Not at all."

"But I won't use the money only for me. I want to help the creatures."

He grunted. "I'm not seeing the connection."

"Throughout my life, pets have kept me going. I adopted a stray kitten on the space station, and my mom let me keep her. When I was older, I volunteered at the station's creature shelter. My goal is to donate a good portion of the prize money to them so they can continue to place beasties in loving homes."

"That's admirable, Wren."

"Kind of goes with the name, you know?"

"A wren was a variety of bird on Earth."

"I don't think they're extinct yet." I grunted. "Now that I've spilled my guts, what about you? I'm sure you're salivating about that catering job too."

"I own a restaurant on my home planet. My goal is to use the catering job to give my career a big boost."

"I assume the money will help with that boost, plus give you more to support your sister."

"Exactly. She'll be released from rehab soon, and if I win, the money will let me hire staff to aid in her transition to living independently. I can afford to give her most of what she needs, but it's tight. I've used up most of my savings already."

"You're a good brother."

"I've tried."

I chuckled. "Like my mom, I guess, except I can tell you're succeeding. I always wondered . . ."

"What?"

"If she'd stayed with me at the space station, would she have one day succeeded?"

"It's good to think she would've."

"I hope so. It's been more than ten years since I saw her. When I'm older and less than half of my life has been spent with her, I might change my mind about that." It was nice to think it would've happened. That was my dream for so long, that she'd get a job, find us a better place to live, and snub her nose at the world around us. "I'll prove we're good people for her."

"Wren." He hugged me, and there was nothing wrong with absorbing some of the sympathy he so readily offered. It wasn't stealing if it was freely given. "It sounds like we both have a lot to lose if we don't finish first."

"Maybe neither of us will win. Omyn might scoop up the prize."

"If that's the case, we'll both keep limping along, doing the best we can," he said.

It would crush me to return to the station to either beg for my old job or find another, but I'd do it with my chin lifted. I'd made it onto Interstellar Chef. There was no shame in not finishing first. At this point, if I still had my arms intact, I'd call it a win.

"You're right. We will." He inhaled and released a long sigh, followed by a yawn. "I think we should get some rest, don't you?"

"You said you were going to tell me a story. I always enjoy a good tale before bedtime." I said it half in jest, but he didn't laugh.

"It *is* a good story," he finally said.

I settled back in his arms as he started speaking.

14
THROM

"My parents died when I was eighteen and my sister three. I raised her," I said.

"How did they die?"

"A shuttle accident. They went on vacation, leaving me to watch my sister, but they never made it home."

"Wow. I'm sorry." She leaned back in my embrace. "We've both had to step up and be braver than we feel."

She was right. At the time, I didn't see it as brave. "I just did what I had to."

"Which was brave. You could've handed her off to someone else to raise."

"No way. We were family. We were all the other had left."

"See? Brave," she said like she'd proven her point.

"Anyway, I got a job in a restaurant and slowly started learning how to cook."

"Like me," she said, and I heard joy in her voice. I also liked that we shared this in our past.

"The owner must've seen potential in me because he started training me. He'd studied under some of the most illustrious chefs, and he taught me all I know. When he died, he surprised me by leaving me the restaurant."

"And here you are, competing in Interstellar Chef to give yourself a boost up in the cooking world."

"Exactly. I was incredibly lucky."

"You earned it."

"What do you mean?"

"He didn't pick you off the street and hand you the business. You earned the right to claim it."

I'd never seen it like that, but she was right.

Wren had no mentors, no one to look out for her other than herself. It was clear she'd cared for her mother despite her parent's flaws, but my gut burned with anger.

A parent should do the best they could for their child. A young female shouldn't be forced to fend for herself. But Wren's story wasn't uncommon. Many adults got addicted to drugs, or couldn't do what they should, despite the desire to do so. When children grew up in a household like that, many would wind up just like their parents.

Wren found a way out, which spoke to her strength. Her determination.

I respected her so much, and I'd soon tell her. But she kept yawning, and her head bobbed forward. She needed rest.

"Sleep. I'll watch out for us both," I said.

"When are you going to rest?"

I loved the sound of sleep in her voice. What would it be like to wake up with her in my bed, in my arms, and hear her say good morning in the same voice?

Pure bliss.

"I'll sleep on the prince's ship while it's transporting us to the next location."

"Why don't I sleep for a few hours, and then you can wake me. You can sleep after that."

"I can handle this, Wren," I growled, though I wasn't irritated with her.

"Like you did when you were eighteen and your parents died. But I'm not three. I can step up at your side. No need for me to hang out in your shadow."

She was too damn perceptive.

I wanted to protect her, but after what she'd told me of her past, it was clear she could protect herself. She was fiercely independent, first by habit, and then by choice. The last thing she needed was for me to step in and do things for her.

"I'm sorry." How could I grumble when she made perfect sense? "You're right. I'll wake you."

"Thank you." She started to scoot forward, but I held her back.

"Where are you going?"

"Well, I have to pee, though I don't believe I'll be able to do it up here."

"You could squat and . . ."

"Let it run downhill?" she said with a laugh. "*You're* downhill."

"I could help you . . . um . . . hold position." It wasn't easy for me to delicately state something like that.

"That would sound creepy if I didn't know you better." She flashed me a grin over her shoulder. "If you turn your back, I'll find a way to do this without falling off the branch or sending unwanted streams in your direction."

"I'll, um, stay here."

She eased away from me and started crawling along the branch. "Eyes closed, Throm. No peeking at my ass."

"It's a cute ass." I hadn't gotten it out of my mind since I first saw it.

"If you want a peek, you'll have to wait until the time is right."

At least she was offering that. "I can wait." Forever if I had to.

When she'd finished, she returned and settled in front of me. "If you need to pee, go for it. Guys can squirt wherever they please."

I chuckled. "It does come in handy."

In no time, I joined her in my original place, behind her with my back to the trunk, her tight in my arms. She stretched her legs out on the branch in front of her.

"Sleep," I said in a lulling voice.

"Thanks."

"For telling you to sleep?"

She tapped my arm that tightened around her. "You know what I mean."

"I do, but there's no need to thank me. We're in this together."

"Sort of. For now, right? If we make it to the last round, we'll have to toss our friendship aside."

That was something I'd never be able to do.

I didn't want to lose, and I would try my hardest to win. But if I finished first, I'd take the money she could use to buy herself a new life. And make life harder for the pets she was determined to save.

A person couldn't buy a reputation.

It was a dilemma, and I didn't have any answers.

15
WREN

Just as I'd asked, he woke me partway through the night. While he slept—and lightly snored—I turned sideways on the branch, holding him steady while watching the leaves around us flutter in the wind. Creatures moved across the forest floor, some lumbering without fear, others tiptoeing so quietly, if I hadn't looked down, I would've missed them.

I held my breath when something swung through the trees, passing not far from us. It didn't pause, so it either didn't know we were here, or it didn't care.

By morning, my legs were asleep. I had to move.

With care, I eased away from him. His arms flopped down onto his thighs, but he didn't appear at risk of falling.

I turned to face him, lowering my legs over one side. My butt ached from sitting on the hard surface.

"Hey," he said, his eyes opening.

There was nothing sexier than this guy in the morning.

He gave me a lazy smile and lifted me effortlessly, placing me on his lap with my legs on either side of his hips.

"This is an intimate position," I said, unable to avoid noting he had a morning stiffy. Totally a guy thing. Like, the sun rose, and their cocks did along with it.

"What are you going to do about this *intimate* position?" he asked, sliding his hands along my lower back. The gesture could be read as a seductive caress or him just making sure I didn't fall off his lap.

"What *should* I do?" I asked, waiting for his cue.

"Whatever you please." His eyelids were hooded, and he focused on my mouth, making my lips heat up. Other parts too.

"We're not supposed to get touchy-feely."

"You're right. No fraternization. It's in the rules."

"There aren't camera bots watching us now."

"Where are you taking this, Wren?" he asked in all seriousness. His body stilled as if my answer meant a lot. "Spell it out for me."

"I'm taking it here." I rose and placed my lips on his, lightly in case he wanted to turn away.

He did anything but. He tightened his hold on my back, pulling me fully against him. Like the night we met, I could feel his cock pressing between my legs. Like then, I wanted to feel him buried deep inside me.

I wasn't going to take things that far. We'd started out this way, and I'd crashed and burned when he'd left. We'd just reconnected. I'd be a fool to try to build a relationship with sex.

Still, I couldn't stop rubbing against him. And when our mouths broke apart, and he fed me a sexy grin, I slid down his body and started rocking against his cock.

He held my hips and watched me, letting me lead this wherever I chose to take it.

His fingers strayed up my sides, pausing on the outer

part of my breast. I turned my upper body toward his hand, seeking his touch.

With a groan, he slid his hand beneath my shirt and cupped my breast. His fingers glided across the nipple, bringing it to a hard bud in seconds.

While I pumped against him, wishing I could throw away my inhibitions, impale myself on him, and ride him until we both exploded, I wasn't going to do it.

This was crossing the line enough for me now.

"You're so sweet when you're aroused, Wren," he growled. "I want to see you like this all the time."

"How about when I'm cooking?" I quipped. Frankly, it was all I could do to focus on conversation. His cock was thick and long, and it was a tease to have clothing between us.

His hand slid down from my breast to the top of my elastic-waisted pants. He dipped a finger beneath the waistline, stroking across my skin, while watching my face for approval or rejection.

"Touch me," I demanded. I was a greedy thing, wanting everything all at once. It probably came from my upbringing when I had nothing. Now that the buffet, so to speak, was spread out before me, I wanted to gorge myself until I popped.

He took care with his claws when he inched his hand inside my pants, and it was good that he did. I was so lost in the moment; I didn't care if I had to walk to the prince's spacecraft without anything on below my chef's tunic.

When he touched my clit, I lost all control. I moved against him, whimpering while he rubbed.

I latched onto his horns, and he groaned, tipping his head back. His eyelids closed, and he panted.

"I'm not hurting you, am I?" I asked

"Don't stop. I didn't realize . . . I'd heard it could happen, but I didn't think . . ."

"What?" To test things, I stroked my fingertips up and down his horns, riding the coils from where his horns left his head to the tips.

His guttural groan rang out, and he pumped his hips hard against me.

Quizzing him about this could come later. It was time to feel.

We rocked together, our ragged breathing echoing around us. Each time I thrust forward; it pushed his finger hard against my clit while his cock ground against my open slit. I was dripping wet, and that made everything slippery.

He carefully inserted his knuckle inside me, moving it in and out. His other hand slid into my pants and took over rubbing my clit.

I was a hurricane flinging itself toward the shore. A volcano about to erupt. A wanton woman who wanted to grind against the hottest alien she'd met in her life.

In no time, I was a wreck, bucking and moaning as I rushed toward my release. When it came, it rocked me to my core, and his echoing groan tingled down my spine. I moved harder against him, feeling the connection between us deepening. His gaze never left mine, and I swore awe filled his eyes.

I needed him, and it wasn't just about sex. Sure, I wanted to ride this for as long as it would stay with me, needing to do the same for him. But with each of his thrusts against me, and each time his finger moved deep inside, I felt the bond we'd created an interstellar year ago expanding. It sucked me in and there was nothing I wanted more than to fall. He'd catch me. Always. I knew this within my soul.

I wasn't sure I liked letting emotions slip into this. Life was easier when you didn't care.

Yet Throm was someone to stand beside. To fight for. And I couldn't seem to stop myself from getting involved.

He finished with a heady groan, shuddering.

I collapsed against him, totally spent.

He rubbed my back while I gently stroked his horns.

I fell asleep in his arms.

And I woke to someone calling my name.

16

THROM

"Hello?" someone called, their voice echoing through the forest. "Thrombuka? Wren? Are you alive?"

"We're here," I called.

"Do you need help? Are you safe?" they asked.

I couldn't see them, but from the rustle of brush, they called from someplace near the ship.

"We're okay," Wren said. She shot me a shy smile. "More than okay, if I do say so myself."

"So much more," I said, leaning forward to kiss her.

"Where are you?" they called.

"We're up in a tree," I bellowed. "We'll come to you."

I stood, holding Wren in my arms, and she slid down my front to touch her feet on the branch.

"Your pants are wet," she said, cringing as she glanced down. "I'm sorry."

I chuckled, though I wouldn't be laughing when I walked, and things rubbed. "I wouldn't undo what happened between us for anything, Wren."

Watching her fall apart and doing the same in her arms

was the best thing that had happened in my life. My mate. I couldn't claim her yet, but I would soon.

When this was over and things had settled, I would tell her I'd sought her for the past year. That I wanted to build a forever. The affection I felt for her would continue to grow, and I wanted the chance to build something wonderful between us.

Would telling her my thoughts make her run away? I didn't wish to scare her. But the thought of saying goodbye, of each of us going in a different direction, made me feel like I took a blade in the chest. I couldn't breathe, and I didn't want to if she wasn't sharing my life.

She climbed onto my back, and I took us to the ground after making sure no vines lurked in the area.

A snap to our left sent me spinning, but I didn't see anything there. I'd watch our backs though until we were safe with the others.

While we'd walked for some time the night before, we weren't far from the clearing where the toxin-filled shuttle still waited.

We emerged from the jungle to find everyone standing near a ship that had to be four times as big as the one we'd arrived in.

This was a simple day-cruise vessel?

Omyn's narrowed gaze flicked between us, but my tunic covered the evidence—I'd made sure of that before we walked into view.

Crik'ee chatted with the pilots of our shuttle and the prince's, his arms now equal in length.

"There you are," Crik'ee said, looking our way. "We were wondering where you'd disappeared to."

"I hoping they dancing with vines," Omyn said in a low

voice that was just loud enough for us to hear but not loud enough that anyone could scold him for being nasty.

Almost anyone.

"Omyn," Crik'ee said, frowning at the other chef. "Don't be like that."

"You want another arm rip off?" Omyn snarled at Crik'ee.

"No. I like my arms." Crik'ee scurried around to the other side of the pilots, whipping his arms behind his back.

We joined the pilots.

"If you're ready to leave?" the prince's pilot said. "I'm .. . Dekrin, by the way."

I wasn't sure why his gaze darted away from mine. It hardly mattered. The prince would not employ anyone unless they were fully vetted.

"I've been directed to fly you to the next few destinations," he said.

"Thank you," I said, taking in his height equal to mine and his similar build. His dark purple skin almost sparkled in the sunlight, and his black hair threaded with silver bands had been pulled back at the nape of his neck.

He nodded. "Always happy to help. I don't get to travel as often as I'd like."

"The prince doesn't take many day trips?" Wren asked, striding around to stand beside Dekrin. I imagined she did so to put space between us. What we'd shared in the jungle took us perilously close to the edge. We couldn't let anyone discover the emotions growing between us.

"If you would all board the craft," Dekrin said. "I'll show you to your cabins and we can get going." He dipped his head to the other pilot. "You're sure you're comfortable remaining here with the ship?"

"I've got this," she said, hefting the pistol. "And I'll climb to the top of the craft."

"All right," Dekrin said.

"The repair crew should be along shortly." She looked at her com. "Once my ship is safe to board, I'll fly the ship to a repair dock where they can replace the vent system and make sure this doesn't happen again."

As she waved, we climbed up the ramp and into the prince's ship. The hatch closed behind us.

"There are cabins on either side of the hallway," Dekrin said, waving in that direction. "They're all the same, and each has its own personal sanitizer. The room at the end of the hall is a suite, but it belongs to the prince. It's locked, and it'll remain that way for the entire time you're on board."

In other words, don't try to enter. I had no problem with that.

"There is also a fabricator in each room," he said. "It won't generate a ball gown," his nod took in Wren, "but it'll create simple clothing."

"I'm fine without a gown," Wren said with a wry twist of her mouth.

"And if you're hungry," the pilot said, "the last door on the right is a small galley. You'll find simple pre-prepared meals and beverages in the small chiller, plus a synthesizer to make whatever else you might like to eat. Feel welcome to use the facilities. The prince sends his regards and his wish for you to enjoy your journey."

"Thank you," Wren said, and the rest of us echoed her words.

"I'll be on the bridge preparing for takeoff. If you have questions, please don't hesitate to find me." He smiled, revealing fangs. "I'm always up for a good conversation." He turned and strode toward the front of the ship.

Omyn and Crik'ee rushed down the hall and entered the first two rooms on the right. Wren and I followed, her taking the first on the left and me the second.

I stepped inside my room and locked the panel, grinning in appreciation at the decent-sized bed, the synthesizer unit sitting on a shelf, and the entrance to a big sanitizer on my right. A wide window allowed me to look out at the jungle. It would be nice to lie in bed and watch the ship fly past the stars.

It was only when I'd dragged my tunic over my head in preparation of using the sanitizer that I noticed a door on my left.

I walked over to it and swung it open.

"Oh," Wren said. She stood by an equal-sized bed, completely naked, her hands covering her breasts. "Ever think of knocking first?"

17
WREN

"Adjoining rooms, eh?" I said with a wry twist of my lips. It was silly to feel shy after what we'd done in the jungle, but there it was. "I don't suppose there's a lock on my side?"

"You'd lock me out of your room?" He sounded affronted, but really.

"That's not the point, Throm. No fraternization rule?"

He couldn't take his gaze off my body. "I'm sorry." His words came out with a groan. "You don't have any clothing on."

"Because I was about to step into the sanitizer and remove the sweat and grime from my body." I released a breast and pointed to the door. "Out."

"But—"

"Out."

"You're right." He dipped forward in a short bow. "I apologize. I will not open this door again unless you ask me to."

Which I might. This morning had been an appetizer. I was still hungry for the full meal.

"We have to be careful," he added, backing into the opening.

"The show will be over in a few days."

"You are correct. A few days, and we can talk."

I wasn't sure what he planned to discuss. Where did he see this going between us? It was clear he wanted my body, but what about me? I was a full-package kind of girl, especially now that my heart had decided it might be enjoying the game.

He closed the door softly, and while I didn't hear the click of a lock, I was confident he wouldn't boldly stride inside my room again without giving me a chance to cover up first.

I stepped into the sanitizer and let it do its thing while my brain whirled, though I didn't have any answers for my multitude of questions.

"Finish this contest first," I whispered as I dressed in jeans and a tee after I was clean. "Win, and then . . ." I guess we'd figure that out when the time came.

We'd?

When had I started thinking of me and Throm as a pair?

Sighing, I left my room and strode to the kitchen, where I fixed a plate and sat at a tiny table to consume my meal.

Omyn joined me, taking the seat across from mine.

The last thing I wanted was to chat with a six-armed alien who enjoyed ripping off his competitor's arms.

He grunted while he ate. After he was done, he sat back and sighed, patting his belly while staring at me. "You need be careful.'

"In what way?"

"Camera bots everywhere."

"Not here. They're also not in our rooms." Or so I was told. I needed to look around. I'd downloaded a—not quite legal—app to my com some time back that could locate hidden cameras. I'd check my room and the public areas of the ship as soon as I'd finished eating.

"You is correct," he said. "None in rooms." He rose and dropped his plate into the small processor sitting near the synthesizer, then headed toward the hall. But he stopped before he left the small room, turning back to face me. "Camera bot near shuttle this morning."

"What do you mean by that?"

"You and Thrombuka in forest together during night."

"Crik'ee and the pilot were in the forest together all night too."

"You and Thrombuka not wit Crik and pilot during night." A slick grin rose on his face. "I ask."

"All of us couldn't fit on one branch, so we found another tree nearby." Nearby was a stretch, but I didn't need to be honest with him. I stood, though the added height didn't make a lot of difference when compared to a seven-foot-tall hulking alien. "We hid in the tree while vines and creatures stalked us all night. It was terrifying."

He chuckled.

I scowled. "I'm not sure what you're suggesting, but—

"Not suggest any-ting. Saying camera bots watching. They see every-ting." His grin widened, revealing jagged rows of teeth. The front set were the longest, and I'd read his species could bite through bone with barely a crunch. "Me see too."

Turning, he strolled into the hall.

I slumped into my chair and fiddled with what was left of my food. Just because a camera had filmed us this morning, didn't mean it had followed us into the woods last night. We were told we'd get a break from being on stage when the show wasn't running.

But they *had* outlined the rules and hooking up was definitely off-limits. Shit, if the bots saw us . . .

They couldn't have. If they'd filmed me gyrating against Throm's cock, we would've been booted off the show already.

A chill tracked through me, and I wrapped my arms around my waist, shivering. I'd lost my appetite.

I got up and dumped my plate, then practically ran to my room. A quick sweep with my app revealed my room wasn't bugged. Neither were the outer hall and kitchen. Damn Omyn playing with my mind. This ship belonged to the prince. His staff would ensure he was safe from spying.

The shuttle we'd arrived in might be bugged, however, and I'd have to be careful if we were shuffled back to that craft after the next event.

Assuming I made it through the next round and wasn't eliminated from the show.

No, I had to remain confident. I was an excellent chef. Everyone raved about the meals I prepared. I'd won awards.

I could win this if I maintained my focus on what was most important.

So much was at stake here. We weren't playing silly games. Only one of us was going to win and claim the prize many chefs would kill to obtain.

I didn't think Throm was fooling around with me, however. He liked and desired me, and he came across as a completely honest person.

But I needed to be careful, or I could lose not just money for the creature shelter.

I could ruin the bit of good reputation I'd built since my mom ditched me.

18

THROM

I didn't see Wren during the flight to our next destination, but I assumed she was sleeping. We'd barely slept the night before, and yesterday was stressful. I took a nap myself.

The prince's ship took us to our next destination, the floating islands of Fistella. Late in the day, the craft landed on the largest island, and we got off, staring around in awe at the pale purple sky dotted with puffy, light pink clouds, the dark lavender grass beneath our feet, and the lush vegetation in all colors of the rainbow growing in perfusion around us.

Smaller islands hovered nearby, and, from what I'd read, no one had been able to figure out why they didn't fall, since this planet had normal gravity. Other parts of the planet contained mountains and deserts like other worlds, but this section was made up solely of the floating bits of land with a vast ocean teeming with sea life far below.

The ship's engines fired, and the craft lifted off behind us, flying toward the outer atmosphere and leaving us alone on the large island.

I joined Wren as she stood off to the side, taking everything in while enjoying just being near her.

A camera bot whizzed past, pausing to film us both.

Wren visibly shuddered, watching until it zipped over to Omyn to showcase his gruesome smile. Dancing for whoever might soon be watching, he played it up for his fans. When the camera moved on to Crik'ee, Omyn looked our way and cackled.

Wren grimaced and shot me a frown. Without saying anything, she strode over to stand with Crik'ee, who hopped in place and pointed at one thing after another, squealing periodically and totally ignoring the camera.

I didn't like that they were watching us already, but the show needed to keep viewers happy. Happy viewers meant high bids for hot spots by sponsors.

Wren and I would be careful. I wouldn't endanger her chance at winning, though she'd only do so through her own merits.

She didn't look my way, and I scratched the back of my neck, starting to get worried. Was she avoiding me?

I could've said something I shouldn't have. Ah, yes. I'd stupidly walked into her room without knocking first. I'd caught her naked—a stunning view I saw each time I closed my eyes.

But it had been a rude move. I'd apologized, but it appeared I was going to have to make it up to her in another way.

My body had some great ideas, but I shut it down fast. I'd find a different way to show her I was sorry.

Jell's personal transport pod soared across the sky and landed not far away. He disembarked and zipped over to join us on his personal hover jet. "Welcome contestants." His gaze took in the three suns sinking down toward the horizon and the surrounding beauty. "Since you've arrived late in the day, we'll wait until tomorrow for the next event."

A small shuttle landed near Jell's pod and staff started unloading supplies.

"Tonight, you'll sleep in tents," he said. "Cramping, I believe they call it on Earth."

Wren snorted but said nothing.

"Why not prince ship?" Omyn asked.

Jell frowned before continuing. "It will orbit the planet for now but will return when we need it. You'll board and wait for the winner to savor their prize before it takes you on to the third event. Those who are not booted off the show, that is. For tonight, our amazing audience will be fed a live stream of you four cramping."

"I hope not," Wren whispered.

"Do you have something to share?" Jell asked her.

She shook her head. "This is such a lovely place. I can't wait to . . . cramp here."

"You are correct. It is lovely." Jell flew over to speak with the staff setting up four tents, placing mattresses and odds and ends inside each.

I walked over to Wren. "Do you have a moment to talk?" I asked in a low voice.

Crik'ee glared at me. "She was conversing with me."

Wren carefully turned her back to me and engaged Crik'ee. "Do you know much about this planet? I find it amazing." Her hand swept out. "Look at the smaller islands. They seem to hover in the air, but I don't see how it's scientifically possible."

"Well," Crik'ee said, his voice lifting. "As you know, no one understands why the islands do not fall into the sea. There are no wires suspending them, and no one had found a means of propulsion on the underside, which," his arm swept out to the islands nearby, "as you can see, the bottoms show dangling roots. Dirt literally falls off if they are bumped. The islands remain stationary, however, so there will be no bumping together while we are on them."

"Do you think we'll compete on one of them tomorrow?" she asked, appearing utterly fascinated with everything Crik'ee had to say.

I could've told her all this. I wanted to share the wonder of this world with her. But for some inexplicable reason, she wasn't interested in sharing it with me.

I wanted to huff and stomp my feet like a youngling, but that would be foolish. She was welcome to speak with whomever she pleased.

I'd pin her down later and ask if there was something wrong.

"If you'll gather around again," Jell said. "I'll fill you in on what to expect next. Drones will prepare a meal for you tonight and in the morning."

The drones were already at work, setting up a small cooking station where they'd craft our meal.

"As for tomorrow's event," Jell said, zipping back and forth in front of us to ensure he held the viewers' attention. "You will compete with each other to prepare the best evening meal possible. We'll provide exciting options that are grown or produced only on Fistella."

I was curious about the mystery ingredient as well as what the cooking set-up would be. Yesterday, they'd kept things simple with everyday stations. I wasn't confident this pattern would continue. It never had in prior shows.

"Do you have any questions?" Jell asked.

We shrugged.

"Very well, then," he said. "Remember to give our audience an enticing show tonight!" He hoverjetted to his pod and climbed inside. It soon soared toward the sky, taking him to his waiting ship where he'd relax for the night in splendor.

Wren went over to watch the drones prepare dinner, and as soon as they started plating, she took one and went into her tent to eat, closing the canavar door flap behind her.

I joined the other guys around the chemfire one of the drones lit. So much for hanging out, staring at the flames with Wren, while pointing out constellations.

Night fell, and I remained by the fire even after Crik'ee and Omyn went inside their tents. I kept hoping Wren would come out and we could talk. I wouldn't press her about us, but I wanted to be near her. I was heartsick, and I didn't know what to do about it.

I didn't go to her tent. I stayed away, respecting what I perceived as her need for distance. We'd talk eventually, but not near the camera bots. They wouldn't be on us all the time.

Eventually, I went to bed, though I slept restlessly on the koofa mattress. I got up early and emerged from the tent, hoping to find a quiet moment to speak with Wren before the others joined us.

I wanted to tell her I wouldn't push this, that we could wait until the contest was over, that I wouldn't come between her and her chance to win.

Her tent flap remained closed.

By the time the drones had cooked breakfast and plated a meal for each of us, she still hadn't emerged.

I took a plate from a drone and strode to her tent. This was silly. She needed to eat, and she needed to come out and join us. We weren't the only ones the camera bots wanted to record.

I scratched on her tent flap, but she didn't call out.

When I stooped down and tucked my head inside her tent, I found it empty.

19
WREN

So, I was a coward.

Once everyone went to bed, I dragged a few blankets from my tent and my pillow, and I strode through the purple grass to the edge of the floating island. I didn't mind heights, but we had to be miles in the air, so I didn't get close enough to look down.

Dropping to the grass, I spread out a blanket and lay on my back, covering myself with the other blanket.

I watched the stars—a bunch of them shot across the sky—and I drifted to sleep.

I woke to pandemonium.

"Wren. Wren!" Throm cried, desperation lifting his voice.

"Wren," Crik'ee wailed. "Did you hurt her, Omyn?"

"Me?" Omyn cried. "Eliminate with cooking, not outside contest."

Crik'ee huffed. "You'd eviscerate one of us if you thought you could get away with it."

"She kidnapped," Omyn bellowed. "Kidnapped! Take by

slavers. Sold. Gone forever. Now only two left for show, plus me."

Footsteps slammed past where I lay tucked beside a bush. I must've rolled here during the night, taking my top blanket with me. The grass felt fluffy beneath me, like I laid on a down comforter. I'd never felt down in any form, but I'd read about it and could picture how it would be to lie on top of it.

"I'm here," I said, sitting up.

Throm skidded to a stop. He dropped to his knees and started to gather me into his arms. At least, I assumed that was what he was going to do.

I kinda hoped he'd kiss me while he was at it. I'd stayed away to make this easier for us both but avoiding him sucked big hairy balls. I'd missed him, and he was just outside my tent. I'd heard him moving about near the fire long after Crik'ee and Omyn went to bed, and it was all I could do not to leave my tent and seek him out. I'd wanted to curl up in his arms.

I was falling fast and despite my determination not to let him into my heart, to hold myself back until the show was over, I was a goner already.

What sucked even more was that I couldn't do anything about it.

The camera bot hovering to my right proved that point.

"Are you all right?" he asked in a low voice filled with the same longing piercing me.

"I'm sorry I worried you."

He stood and offered to help me stand before pressing his palm against his thigh.

I'd seen what he did, the bots, plus the other guys watching us from across the open area could have. Even the drones who'd prepared our meals could be spying.

There was no place safe for us to talk, let alone kiss.

Still, no one said we couldn't be friends, so I held out my hand.

He flashed me a quick smile, relief spilling across his face, before smoothing his mouth into a neutral expression.

With his help, I rose to my feet. I grabbed my blankets, and we walked back to the "cramping" area.

"You missed out on a great breakfast," he said softly.

I watched as the camera bots zipped ahead of us. Jell had arrived, and for now, he'd provide more entertainment than me and Throm.

"I want you to cook for me some time," I said. "Would you do that?"

"I'd love to." He flashed me another smile. "I'm sorry if I've made things awkward."

It stung that he was trying hard to make things right between us when, so far, he'd done nothing wrong.

"I'm sorry I avoided you," I said, keeping my voice low. A glance around showed we were alone, Omyn and Crik'ee striding ahead to meet up with Jell. "I don't want to." There was so much more I wanted to say, but we still had to be careful.

He nodded. "We'll find time tonight to talk."

Talk? I wanted more of what he'd given me this morning.

But I just couldn't figure out how we could snatch a moment away together where no one could catch us doing something we shouldn't.

20

THROM

"All right, everyone," the producer bot called out. "Showtime in ten . . . Nine . . ."

Jell grinned. "Ready!"

"And one . . ."

"Welcome back to Interstellar Chef, the competition of the multi-universe," Jell cried, zooming up into the sky on his hover jet with camera bots following like loyal pets. He did a back flip, then flew down to soar across the front of us where we stood waiting. We'd changed in our tents into new outfits, the tunics emblazoned with the show's logo.

Two camera bots hovered within a few inches of my face, and I noted other bots near Wren, Omyn, and Crik'ee.

I girded myself for the upcoming reveal. Our viewers would be eager to catch the shock on our faces when they revealed the mystery ingredient or where or how we were expected to prepare it.

I caught Wren's gaze, and she gave me an encouraging nod. I did the same, enjoying that while we were competitors, we also supported each other.

Crik'ee bobbed back and forth from his toes to his heels,

staring around wildly. He kept his arms tight to his sides, however, especially the one next to Omyn.

"Don't see stations," Omyn said with a frown, scanning the area.

I'd already searched the entire island and found nothing but vegetation and a few ground creatures the size of birds that had scooted away when I came near.

"Impatient, impatient," Jell said with a grin, shaking a scolding finger Omyn's way. "Welcome fans, welcome contestants. Are you ready for the second event of the season?"

The fake audience screamed.

We nodded.

Jell grimaced and flicked his hand our way, keeping it below camera level.

"I can't wait," Wren shouted with a grin.

The rest of us joined in, telling Jell we were unbelievably excited. Anything to get this going. My nerves were shot and not only because of the event. I worried about me and Wren and how we'd make this work.

"What's up for today, you ask?" Jell said. "Well, for today's event, our remaining illustrious chefs will prepare . . ." He grinned, enjoying making us—and the rest of the multi-universe who would soon watch the recorded show—wait, "A dinner course!"

Dinner sounded good. It gave the judges more than one or two items to base their final decision on.

Wren's grin told me she felt the same.

Jell chuckled as the fake audience cheered. "I'm as eager as our chefs are to see what the producers have . . . cooked up for the mystery ingredient." He snickered at his joke. "Would you like to see where they'll compete among the floating islands of Fistella?" He cocked his head and grinned. "I can't hear you."

The audience roared to drive those watching into a frenzy.

Jell did another back flip before stopping his hover jet a short distance away from us.

"For today's event, you will each prepare a meal on one of the floating islands," he shouted. "Be aware that each island holds its own *interesting* features, though they've all been scored to ensure they offer equal challenges." He flashed us a big smile. "Would you like to get started, chefs?"

"Yes," Crik'ee cried, bouncing in place and clapping.

"Please board the hover jets behind you, provided by the amazing Wexell Corp, the producer of fine sauces and marinades. If you need to get saucy, buy Wexell!" Jell said.

While the fake crowd roared, I took in the hover jet that had landed behind me.

"Once you've been secured in your hover jet," Jell said, "the device will take you to your individual island. All aboard."

We stepped onto the hover jets and waited while they molded around our feet and lower legs. The fusion would provide stability while the devices flew, though good balance was also essential. You couldn't fall from them, they didn't allow for that, but you could take a wild, frightening ride if you didn't relax your body and allow for the hover jets usually smooth movements.

Wren sent me a frown as she stepped onto hers.

I quietly called out instructions, though the camera bots would pick up every word I said. There was nothing in the rules stating helping a fellow competitor was forbidden.

Crik'ee yelped when the jet fused around his ankles, but Omyn stared forward blandly.

The hover jets lifted off, and we soared across the rest of this island and out over the enormous sea churning far below.

"Wow, look at that," Wren said, shooting a wry smile my way. She pointed to the water shimmering in the sunlight. "It's beautiful here. Amazing. I'd heard about the floating islands, but I never thought I'd see them."

"It truly is gorgeous. There are resorts on some of the larger islands, though not in this area, and the cost of staying is beyond almost everyone's means, but that's the point. They only cater to the most exclusive clientele."

Our hover jets split, making it hard to carry on a conversation without shouting, and I studied the small islands peppering the area, some completely overgrown with trees, others stark and bare. A few gleamed like they were made of precious stones, while others contained only rocky outcroppings. Most were smaller than the island where we'd spent the night. What could I expect in this round of competition?

My hover jet approached a tiny island with barely enough room to stand. A cooking station had been set up, and boxes had been placed beneath it. This was it?

The hover jet landed on the tiny available foot space.

"Please step off the hover jet," a mechanical voice said, and after it unwrapped itself from my legs, merging with the original structure, I did as asked.

The hover jet zipped away from my island, though I assumed it would return after this round ended.

I studied the small space, struggling not to sigh. If I laid down, my head and feet would jut out beyond the edges. Preparing dinner here was going to provide a challenge.

To my right, Wren's hover jet dropped her off on an island the size of a medium spaceship. Dense vegetation covered most of the surface, though they'd cut away some in the front and placed her cooking station there.

She shrugged my way before peering at the bushes behind her.

To my left, Crik'ee and Omyn had been placed on other islands smaller than Wren's but larger than mine.

I knew each event would present a different but equal challenge. Was my challenge going to be cooking on a small surface without accidentally falling off the side?

Crik'ee stepped toward his cooking station and promptly fell, sliding along the smooth surface of the island, coming dangerously close to the edge. Only a quick grab at one of the legs of his cooking station—that must be secured in place—kept him from a deadly fall. He rose to his feet and bellowed in dismay.

I'd take a tiny cooking space over a slippery floor any day, thanks.

Omyn cackled, looking around what appeared to be a normal island with a grassy ground, a few trees, and sparse spurts of vegetation. He gave me a smug look, grinning about what he perceived as an advantage.

A whirring sound echoed around me as Jell approached.

"Amazing, isn't it, chefs?" He soared up into the sky, startling a cluster of nuleens, creatures with four clawed legs, wings, and long, pointed snouts. They squawked and dove away from his trajectory. He coasted down to hover at our level. "As you can see, there are totes beneath your stations that contain a variety of ingredients that come from this island. No peeking." He chuckled. "Remember, you have forty minues to prepare a complete evening meal.

Don't scrimp on ingredients and remember to use at least three from the totes beneath your stations."

I'd only vaguely heard about what grew and ran about on this planet. Would they keep the ingredients isolated to this region or include almost anything?

"I think it's time to get started, don't you?" Jell said. "I assume you'd like to discover the mystery ingredient?"

All four of us bellowed yes, then waited. I'd wait to view the tote options until I knew what my main ingredient would be.

I girded myself for something to fall from the sky and latch onto my face, though I knew from watching prior shows that each episode would be completely different and unexpected.

A soft sound behind me sent me spinning.

I held onto the cooking station and gaped at what had landed on the ground behind me.

21

WREN

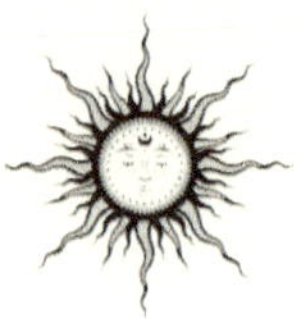

They expected us to prepare a meal that included a marmeek?

The sea creature lay like a blob on the grass-covered ground. With a shrug, I picked it up, cringing as it oozed between my fingers.

I'd read about marmeeks, though I'd never cooked with one before. They were a plant the size of my head and cost more than what I made in a year at my former restaurant—and that *included* tips.

Still, seafood was seafood.

From what I remembered, if you didn't remove the outer membrane, you could poison your diners. And the insides were even more gelatinous than the outside.

I grabbed a bowl and placed the marmeek inside, rinsing it thoroughly to remove any dirt. After I drained away the water, the marmeek sloshed back and forth on the bottom.

Stooping down, I opened the totes beneath my cooking station, examining the options. I wanted to prepare a hearty yet delicate meal, but I had no idea what to make until I saw what I'd been given.

Hmm. Mature, savory gruss could be sauteed in biergart fat to cut the bitterness found in all but baby gruss plants, and the bright purple color would go nicely with the pale pink dotted marmeek.

And if I added . . . *yes*! I placed the strands of gruss on the butcher block set up to the right of my heat conductor and hefted two complete poostards from the tote. I'd have to clean the poostards and pick out the seeds often embedded in the bright yellow flesh. I could use half of each shell, carefully scalloped, as a bowl for a hearty marmeek stew I'd prepare.

I added herbs and spices to my growing pile on the butcher block and dug around in the containers until I found a carton of troolon milk, known for its high butterfat.

And for my side . . . What if I made unleavened nullen wafers the judges could dip into the stew?

It sounded amazing.

I stood and after placing a pan on the heat conductor and setting it to low, I added a glob of biergart fat to melt. I chopped the gruss, tossing it into the pan.

Dropping a saucepan on another burner, I added more biergart fat and chopped oons and spices. While they sizzled, I started carefully removing the poisonous membrane from the marmeek, making sure to toss it well aside and rinse the inner part of the plant thoroughly.

A soft, tittering sound behind me made me turn, but I didn't see anything except the bushes and tall grasses wavering in the breeze on the other side of the island. In preparation of my working here, they'd chopped away the vegetation in an eight-foot circle and placed my cooking surface there. I'd take this station any day over the slippery island Crik'ee had been given.

He appeared to be doing okay, however, carefully moving with his arms splayed wide to maintain his balance.

Omyn's island floated beyond Crik'ee's, and I couldn't see what he was making or how his island provided conflict. If it were me, I'd try to avoid feeling lulled. The surprise trap would spring eventually and being caught unaware could be deadly.

Eyes on my own cooking. That's what would help me win. If I tried to outdo the others, I'd flounder and waste time.

"Thirty minues," Jell cried, floating past each of our islands. "You should know what you're making and have your ingredients prepped already." He paused by my station. "What's on the menu for dinner, chef?"

"A stew and nullen wafers," I said, gliding my fingers across the marmeek to make sure I hadn't missed any membrane.

"It sounds amazing," he said in a chipper voice.

His hover jet flew over to where Throm was perched on a tiny island. Multiple pans had been placed on his cooking surface, and he was busily chopping something orange, though I couldn't tell what it might be.

I added troolon milk to the oons and spices, and turned the burner way down, not wanting to scorch it. I added the finished gruss and after slicing the marmeek into bite-sized chunks, added that. The gelatinous flesh would toughen as it cooked and the outer parts would separate, thickening my broth.

I stooped down to see if there was anything else I could add to my broth to make it pop.

I'd stood and was tossing a handful of brestar nuggets to the broth when caws rang out overhead. A cluster of nuleens swooped down, their claws and pointed snouts extended. They attacked Omyn, pecking his head and flailing upper arms while others plunged toward his back. He swung his arms, knocking some aside, but others landed on his station and started eating the food he'd prepared and plated.

Throm shook his head in dismay but kept working on his meal. Neither of us liked Omyn, but we wouldn't wish this on our worst enemy.

"Twenty-five minues," Jell announced. "You should be starting to think of how you can wrap this up before the time is over!"

Back to work. I had a lot left to do.

I cleaned and cored the poostards, making sure I didn't miss any seeds, then added the flesh to the stew. The larger pieces would remain intact while the pulp would give my broth a savory flavor that would pop when eaten with the wafers.

It didn't take long to mix up the batter for the wafers, and while oil heated in a pan, I rolled out and cut the dough into wedges, plopping each into the oil to cook until they were lightly crispy. The sections puffed like I'd hoped they would, and they started turning golden brown.

Another tittering sound behind me made me pause and frown.

No time. No time!

I pulled the wafers from the oil and laid them on a strip of material to drain.

I still had to scallop the poostard bowls and scorch the inside to give my stew a subtle smoky flavor.

After giving my stew a swirl with a spoon, I attacked the

poostards, carefully cleaning out the rest of the pulpy flesh before slicing along the top to give my bowls an artistic lip.

It was only when something slithered down the back of my leg that I realized I'd been naïve not to wonder why I was given a normal-appearing island.

I turned to find a centivire standing behind me, peering up at me with puzzlement in its eyes. It cocked its head and tittered.

A pack of the lizard-skinned creatures scooted out from the brush on their hind legs. About the size of Earth house-cats, they had vicious claws and long teeth. I'd heard a pack of them could pick a carcass the size of a horse clean within minutes.

They tittered and rushed toward me.

22

THROM

"Fifteen minues left," Jell cried. "Fifteen minues!"

Who cared about that? There was not a damn thing I could do to help Wren except bellow. When she shot a glance my way, I waved a knife, suggesting she grab one fast for defense.

While Omyn swung his arms at the nuleens who continued to swoop and peck him, Crik'ee's feet went out from beneath him and he fell hard on his ass. He wailed and struggled to stand on the smooth surface only to fall again onto his side, hitting his head on the leg of his cooking station on the way down.

I peered around, waiting to see where my threat would come from. A small island was not enough of a challenge when compared to attacking creatures and treacherous surfaces.

As Wren kicked one centivire after another, Crik'ee slowly staggered to his feet. He stared down at what he'd been preparing for his meal and started randomly chopping something green.

Omyn scared away the nuleens and feverishly worked on plating his meal.

"Ten minues," Jell yelled in a cheerful voice. "You should be plating by now, chefs!"

Centivires may be vicious, but they tended to go after carcasses. Sure, they'd been known to take down a person or two, but they preferred easy prey.

Wren slashed the air with a butcher knife, a feral snarl ripping from her lips. When she nicked one of the centivire, the others shrieked. Tittering, they backed away from her. She stomped after them with knives in each hand, screeching. The centivire turned tail and bolted back into the deep grass. Wren pivoted and returned to her station.

"What are you gawking at?" she cried out to me when she caught me watching with my jaw unhinged.

"Just someone kicking centivire ass, sweetheart. Nothing else."

She huffed and returned to her meal preparation, though I caught the pleased smile on her face.

I turned back to my cooking station; confident she could hold her own against anything.

That was when my island tipped to the right. The plates with my gorgeous, creamy flundar sauce slid toward the edge of the butcher block, and the marmeek I'd carefully filleted tumbled off and plopped onto the ground.

I stumbled to the right and stepped squarely on the marmeek.

23
WREN

"Two minues," Jell cried. "You should be putting the final touches on your dishes, chefs!"

I added a sprig of pearlung to the top of my stew to add color to my dish, then carefully laid wedges of nullen beside my lovely, scallop-topped poostard bowls. The rich, savory smell wafting from the stew made my mouth water, reminding me I hadn't eaten since I didn't remember when.

My parched throat protested the lack of water, and my eyelids kept drooping. This is what I got for sleeping outside on the ground. Exhaustion was going to bowl me over soon. I could only hope it came for me after the event was finished, and I hadn't been booted off the show.

Although, if I was kicked off, I'd get the chance to catch up on some Zs.

A glance Throm's way showed him grimacing as he peered at his plates. I couldn't tell from here what he'd made, but my heart had roared up into my throat when his island tipped and everything—including him—went sliding toward the edge. The island had righted itself, but after that, it kept tipping in one direction, then another. As far as I could tell, he'd made the best of the situation.

I'd take centivires any day of the week over an unstable cooking surface.

At least the little beasties hadn't returned to attack.

Jell flew past us on his hover jet, pausing at each station to examine our plates.

"Ah, lovely," he said to me as he passed. He looked at his com and pretended to gasp. "Oh, my. It's nearly time. Three . . . Two . . . One . . . Done!"

We stepped away from our stations. That is, me, Omyn, and Throm stepped away from our stations. Crik'ee slipped and fell, sliding beneath his cooking area. He rose to his knees, clinging to the edge of his station.

"It's time to send your dishes up to our judges," Jell lifted his arm. "Hover beams? Engage!"

Hover beams speared down from the heavens and engulfed my plates. They pulsed, and my dishes shot up toward the waiting judges.

I should be nervous. I'd prepared something simple. But I hoped it was tasty and attractive enough to impress.

"And . . . relax," Jell said, indicating the camera bots had cut to the judges. The bot pestering me settled on the edge of my cooking station and the light on top winked out.

Turning, I watched the woods, not trusting the centivires to leave me alone. But none ventured from the grass, and my pulse slowed.

"I will win," Omyn said with complete confidence. Must be nice to believe in yourself that much. "This one," he nudged his head to where Crik'ee clung to his station, staring around blankly, "did not remove the membrane."

Shit.

"Jell," I cried. "Jell!"

I peered around but couldn't find him.

"Jell," I growled, rounding my table and grabbing the camera bot. I brought it up to eye level and glared at it. "Turn on, damn you."

"What's wrong?" Throm called out from his island, and I explained.

He tipped his head back and bellowed Jell's name, his cries joining in with mine.

Jell must've taken a break on one of the nearby islands.

"Jell." Me and Throm hollered the host's name over and over.

My stupid camera bot wouldn't turn on. Why didn't they watch us during this segment of the game? We weren't cooking but interesting things could be happening.

It was only when Jell soared up from a lower island and flew toward us at a breakneck pace that I knew what must've happened.

He roared down toward Crik'ee, snarling. "You. You!"

Eyes widening, Crik'ee backed away from his station. "What . . . ?"

"You didn't remove the membrane. The membrane," Jell shrieked.

"Membrane." Crik'ee frowned and looked down to where a remnant of his marmeek sat in a forlorn blob. "Marmeek. Membrane." He gazed at us in dawning horror. "I did not remove the membrane."

"You have murdered one of the judges," Jell snarled. He slammed into Crik'ee's chest, sending the Eiy'as male flailing backward. He landed hard near the edge of his floating island.

Crik'ee's feet slipped as he tried to find purchase.

His gaze met mine, and I read a wealth of sorrow there. Blood trickled down the side of his head where a bruise was already forming. We knew they'd throw distractions at us, but I couldn't imagine the horror I'd feel knowing I hadn't focused enough on my work.

Jell smacked into Crik'ee again.

Crik'ee slid off the island and plunged toward the vast sea waiting at least a mile below.

His screams echoed around us until they faded to nothing.

24
THROM

"Crik'ee has been eliminated," Jell said as he soared past the three of us standing on our islands, our jaws dropped in horror. Wren and I expressed horror that is.

Omyn peered over the edge of his island, a slick grin on his face. When he looked up, his smile widened. "Only two left, and I win!"

"With one judge . . . no longer participating in the event, we must wait for another to arrive for the tastings," Jell said.

The camera bots winked out. Convenient that they'd turned on long enough to showcase Crik'ee's fall from his island.

"I am gravely disappointed," Jell said. "You must all be aware of what you are doing. Marmeek is a delicacy, but like many ingredients offered on Interstellar Chef, it comes with inherent danger. If you are unsure about an ingredient, you must speak up. Or ask one of the other contestants."

"Cheating," Omyn cried out. "That be cheating."

"You are allowed to help each other in simple ways like this," Jell said.

Even I knew of that rule. If I'd been on Wren's island, I could've helped her fight off the centivires without either of us being penalized. It would eat into the time I had left to prepare my dishes, but that was the price I'd be expected to pay.

"As I was saying," Jell said, shooting Omyn a scowl. "Speak up if you do not understand something. Either I or one of your fellow contestants—though it is not required—will offer advice."

Omyn's lips squished together, and he shot us glares that dared us to help each other.

Eat shit, Sevest warrior. I'd do whatever I pleased.

"The new judge will, of course, skip Crik'ee's entrée." He scowled at each of us in turn, and even Omyn's arms drooped. "Hover jets will take you to the island where you will wait in the small area prepared for the announcement of today's winner and their prize. After the camera bots have taken in the winner's joy from each angle, and *please*, make sure you express that joy, they will stop filming. The losers will board the spacecraft. After the winner has savored his or her prize for the night, the prince's ship will take you to the next destination." The lines on his pink face deepened. "I warn you. Do not make a mistake like Crik'ee. Everyone knows marmeek membrane is poisonous. *Everyone* removes it before preparing a dish with this ingredient. Everyone asks if they are uncertain."

Crik'ee had made a mistake, but the organizers must realize such a thing could happen. With camera bots watching everything, someone should've picked up on the fact that Crik'ee had not removed the outer marmeek layer. Jell could've zipped over to Omyn and ensured Crik'ee understood how to prepare marmeek. As a last resort, someone should've stopped the judge from sampling the dish.

But ratings meant everything in this show. I was confident the bots watched the judge as they sampled Crik'ee's dish. And I was equally certain they'd flown beside Crik'ee as he fell, not cutting off until he'd disappeared beneath the surface.

The monetary prize was large because of the risk.

My guts wrenched sideways at the thought of an audience watching with glee as Wren was "eliminated."

In most of the shows I'd watched, the losers returned to their home planets, and *not* in body bags. Ratings must be down, so the organizers had opted to heat things up to gain more viewers.

If this was an ongoing plan, no one would agree to compete. Or those like Omyn might, assuming they believed they could survive to the end.

Hover jets approached, and one touched down beside me. I stepped onto the fluid surface, and it released, molding around my feet and lower legs. The device took off, soaring toward the first island with Wren and Omyn's crafts not far behind mine.

A small platform had been set up with a lavender awning fluttering in the breeze. Brightly colored flowers overflowed from the planters placed around the edges of the low platform.

Our hover jets left us near the platform, and we shuffled our feet, watching each other. Omyn could not be trusted; he'd proven that when he attacked Crik'ee. If things came down to another tie, I'd make sure Wren and I were still standing before the show was over.

Wren sagged against a post supporting the platform awning, her eyelids drooping. She couldn't be paying much attention to Omyn, but I'd leap on him if he so much as twitched one claw in her direction.

I wanted to hold her and tell her things would work out fine, but camera bots zipped around us, recording our every expression, and I had no say in the final outcome.

Jell soared over to hover in front of the platform. "We have a winner. We have a winner! Please take places on the platform so we can begin filming. If you can, try to show some emotion." The last, he addressed to Wren.

She rolled her eyes.

We climbed onto the platform and stood in a line. I took the center spot to put space between Wren and Omyn.

Jell plastered a huge smile on his face. "Three . . . Two . . . One!"

Lights flared on the top of the camera bots swirling around us.

"Well, well, well," Jell said. "Welcome back to the final bit of this episode of Interstellar Chef! As you can see, our illustrious chefs are gnashing their teeth, eager to find out who won today's event. Keep your spirits up, chefs. None of you have lost, of course, due to Crik'ee's . . . mishap."

Wren's smile faltered, but she kept her spine tight, and her eyes focused on Jell.

"Would you like to hear what the judges had to say?" Jell asked.

I pumped my fist and let out a warrior's bellow to satisfy the viewers. Wren grinned, baring her teeth.

"Yes, yes," Jell said. "Let's start with . . . Wren." He flew in close to her, his smile widening when he took in the twitch of her lips. "Your stew was well-received. And your wafers? One of the surviving judges composed a brief poem to their exquisite taste, though it will be up to the judge to share it or not. However . . ."

The audience groaned.

"I'm afraid you are not the winner," Jell said pertly.

I growled, having hoped Wren would win this round so she'd be given a night to relax.

"Throm," Jell said, floating over to hover near me. The camera bots blazed, spotlighting me. "One judge would like your recipe for the sauce you made using pureed marmeek. Such an original idea. Inspired. While the other contestants used the marmeek as their main course, sautéing it in Wren's case and grilling it in Omyn's, you chose instead to also use it a more subtle way. Very well done."

It had been crushed beneath my shoe. I had no choice but to clean what was left of the pulp and get creative. At least my quick thinking paid off.

"As for Omyn," Jell said, dipping his head toward the eager Sevest warrior who shifted back and forth on his disproportionate feet. His six arms hung at his side, but he kept flexing his claws. I braced myself to leap on him if he slashed out at me or Wren. "Your grilled marmeek was utter perfection, per one judge, and your use of other ingredients from Fistella truly made the marmeek shine. Kudos for your use of restar toes as a topping. They added just the right crunch to the dish."

Omyn's grin widened.

"Sadly, while I'd like to announce that all three of you have won, our wonderful—surviving—judges have chosen one dish that stood out above them all." He soared into the air with the camera bots zipping along behind him, did a back flip, and returned to hover in front of us, studying each of us in turn. "And now, it's time to announce our winner. Without torturing you further . . ."

A fake drumroll echoed around us followed by the projected roar of a large audience.

Jell's chin lifted. "The winner of this event is Omyn."

25
WREN

While Omyn was whisked away on a hover jet to claim his prize, Throm and I watched each other. With subtle gazes that is. We still needed to be careful.

I was relieved he'd made it through this round, and from the warmth tinged with concern in his eyes, he felt the same about me.

That gave me a squishy feeling inside, and I knew just what I wanted to do about it.

First, however, we had to perform for the viewers.

"I'll win next time, Thrombuka," I snarled. "Watch out. I'm mean with a butcher knife. Hey, Jell. Who came in second place? Please tell me it wasn't this guy." I hooked a thumb toward Throm and snarled. "He dropped his marmeek, you know. I can't imagine it wasn't full of grit from landing on the ground."

Throm's gaze narrowed on me, but when his lips twitched, I knew he'd figure out what I was doing.

"At least I didn't add centivire scales to my dish," he said, his lips curling.

"I never," I cried, huffing loudly for the watching

cameras. "They didn't come close enough for me to scale them, and even if I had, I would've prepared the scales in the correct way. The judges would've raved about their delicate taste and unique flavor."

"Well, well," Jell said, zipping in close to watch our antics. Numerous camera bots followed him, and I assume the future audience would be drinking this up and making bets about who'd get knocked out in the next round. "With you two at each other's throats, I imagine we'll see quite the show during the next event. If I could," he sighed as if heavily put upon, "I'd give you hints about the next location but alas, I'm not allowed to say."

"Oh, pretty please?" I said, injecting a whine in my voice. I grinned at the nearest camera. "I'm ready to leave right now."

Jell's shoulder spikes twitched. "All I'll say . . ."

Another drumroll rang out.

I bit back my sigh, hating all this fake drama.

"All I'll say is that you're going to have to hunt for the mystery ingredient!"

"And cut," the producer bot called out. Camera bot lights went gray, and they soared over to an open metal box and dropped inside.

Drones bustled through the area, picking things up. The show took pride in leaving the location in as close to its original shape as when they arrived.

I sucked in a breath and released it. "I'm glad that's over."

Throm nodded.

Jell directed his hover jet over to his small spacecraft.

"How are we getting off the island?" I called out to him.

"The prince's ship will arrive to collect you shortly. It will orbit the planet until it is time to pick up Omyn in the morning. Don't get into trouble." With a wink, he laid down inside his pod. The lid closed, and the vessel lifted and shot toward the sky.

"What do you think he meant by that?" I whispered, making sure the camera bots had not lifted out of the metal box and that none of the lights had turned back on.

"No idea," Throm said. "I'm tired. How about you?"

"Yeah."

"I was worried when the centivires attacked you."

"And I was worried when your island started tipping. If you'd fallen . . ." I would never get Crik'ee's screams out of my mind.

"We made it through, though. Only two events left."

And that was going to be a problem. Omyn would not accept losing, and if he won the next round, that meant me or Throm would lose. I didn't like the idea of returning to the space station in a sadder situation than when I arrived, but this was about more than money or an exciting job.

I was terrified I'd lose Throm. I'd seen how deadly this show could be, and there was no way I could protect him.

And that's when an idea occurred to me.

It was time to act instead of holding back my longing. A heart softened rarely, and I was ready to hand mine to Throm.

The prince's ship landed, and we strode up the ramp, acting like we were casual friends or adversaries.

"Welcome," Dekrin, the pilot, said with a grin. "Glad to see you've made it to the next round." His gaze shot to the prince's suite at the end of the hall, his eyes widening, but when I looked that way, I didn't see anything. The door was closed like always.

"Thanks," I said. "I'm going to drop onto my bed and sleep a week."

"Well, then," Dekrin said. "I'll get the ship underway. You'll sleep better once I shut the main thrusters down." He flashed us a smile, and even though I lusted after Throm all the time, I wasn't dead. Dekrin was hot.

"Thanks," Throm said.

Dekrin hustled onto the bridge while Throm and I started down the hall.

I stopped outside my door, and Throm paused with me.

With the hatch shut, I could relax. A quick scan with my com's app showed no cameras were watching.

"I can't wait to step into the sanitizer," Throm said. "Then I'm going to take a nap."

With the door shut, I doubted Dekrin could hear, and he didn't seem the type to tattle.

To be safe, I leaned in close to Throm and lowered my voice to a bare whisper. "Would you like company in the sanitizer and with whatever might follow?"

26

THROM

My cock stiffened immediately, a common occurrence around Wren. This wasn't just my body's response to her nearness. No other woman would do. My heart wanted Wren, and it was a greedy thing. It wouldn't be satisfied with anything less than all of her.

I tipped my head toward her room, indicating she should go inside. While she did, I strode to my own. Okay, I ran to my room.

Inside, I shut the door and waited for her to enter through the connecting panel.

She slipped inside my room with a hesitant smile on her face.

She also wore no clothing.

Pure fire ripped through me as I took in her beauty, from her breasts with dark pink nipples I ached to taste, to her lush curves, to the juncture between her thighs I'd do almost anything to explore with my hands and mouth.

"You're drooling," she said with a soft smile. "Is there a dish you'd like to taste?"

"Wren," I choked out, unable to believe this glorious female wanted to be near me.

She strode toward me with a confidence I could only hope to emulate. It humbled me. It made me want to get down on my knees and beg her to be with me always. My heart beat a furious drum in my chest, and my mouth went dry. "I don't think we should be together for long. We can't risk getting in trouble."

I shook my head, still unable to speak.

"But I think we can take a few minues, don't you?" she said.

I nodded.

"Is that a yes?" A shadow of uncertainty passed across her face.

"Yes!"

Her lips twitched upward as she sauntered closer. "You're wearing too much clothing, Throm."

I swallowed and found my voice. "Wren," I choked out.

"Would you rather I returned to my room and sanitized my body there?" She cupped her breasts, lifting them, and stroked her thumbs across the nipples, making them harden to ripe buds. "After, I could take a nap all by myself." Her fingers trailed down her belly.

My cock slammed against the inside of my pants.

I wrenched my tunic off and shoved down the pants, kicking them aside.

I stood before her with my cock on fire, a rigid staff bobbing against my abs, and my heart in my hands. I held my palm out, hoping she'd take it and my heart along with it.

She took my hand in hers and leaned forward to kiss my palm before straightening.

"You've been holding out on me, Throm," she said with

a heady gleam in her eyes. Her gaze traveled down my chest to my abs, and then my cock. "You're a chef, but you appear to work out." Her fingers traced my arms and continued across my chest, pausing to tease my nipples.

"Wren," I said, unable to mutter more than her name. I wanted her more than anything. I'd kill to claim her heart and her soul.

I stroked her shoulders, trailing my fingers down to her pert nipples. When I stroked them, she released a moan. That drove me near the edge, but when I exploded, I fully planned to take her with me.

Leaning forward, I sucked one nipple into my mouth.

"Throm, that feels so good," she said. She tipped her head back, her hair cascading down her back in the lushest of falls, and closed her eyes.

There was nothing more beautiful than watching her face as she succumbed to the pleasure I gave her.

Emboldened, I stroked her other breast while running my tongue across her nipple. She parted her thighs, and nothing would stop me from placing my hand over her mound.

My fingers had claws, but my thumbs did not. I ran one down her wet slit, savoring the fact she was eager for me already.

She moaned deep within her chest and thrust her body toward my hand.

I lifted her and strode to the sanitizer, only pausing when I started to step inside.

"The space is small." Normally, a person stood inside with their legs evenly spread and their arms loose at their sides. They closed their eyes during the process, though their eyes wouldn't be harmed if they remained open. One barely felt the beams that drifted across their flesh, removing dirt and sweat. A light emollient coating drifted down after like a succulent rain. Warmth then flooded the space to ensure the emollient sunk into the person's skin. "I've never stepped inside a sanitizer with another person."

She smiled up at me. "This will be a first for me too. I hope . . ." Color rose in her face, and she dragged her gaze from mine.

"What?"

"I haven't been with a lot of guys. After my mom . . ."

"I'm honored."

"I'm not a virgin," she said with a flash of spunk. "But I'm not very experienced."

"I haven't been with anyone since I met you, Wren. There isn't anyone else I want in my life."

We stood on a precipice. Which way would we fall?

"I can't imagine being with anyone but you, Throm."

And there they were, the words I'd longed for more than almost anything. I truly was humbled that she cared.

When she wiggled, I lowered her to her feet.

She backed into the sanitizer. "Come in here and shut the door, Throm. While I love everything dirty, let's get this over with and find your bed."

Nothing sounded more appealing than that.

I stepped in with her and tugged the door shut.

"I wish there was water," she said. "And soap. I've only cleansed once that way in the past, and it was amazing. I've heard of sitting in tubs or even pools." Bathing with water was mostly unheard throughout the multi-universe other than for the very wealthy.

"If there was water, I'd run my hands all over you," I said in a guttural voice. "And make you come a billion times."

"You're welcome to rub whatever you'd like." She

smiled. "Let's start with one orgasm, shall we? Turn on the sanitizer."

I wasn't sure how this could be sexy, but I was open to exploring everything with Wren.

Pressing the button to engage the device, I closed my eyes and assumed the normal position.

Like always, a subtle breath of air glided across my skin.

Unlike always, a warm hand stroked my cock.

My eyes opened.

"Emollient," she said, stroking me.

She wanted me to think? Nope. I could only feel the emotions cascading through me.

Oh, yes. Emollient. I engaged the next phase of the sanitization process and the system started coating our bodies. But the puff of air to dry us didn't follow. Wren's hands did, gliding across my chest and slipping down my abs. When she grabbed my cock this time, I was well lubricated. Her fingers moved up and down along my body coated with the herbal nutrients that kept my skin soft.

"Wren," I groaned, tipping my head back.

"Do you like this, Throm?"

"Don't stop."

I loved giving her control of my body, of letting her do whatever she pleased. But her tight grip on my cock would send me shooting across the sanitizer within secundas.

"Bed, Throm," she said, and I loved how she directed this as well.

Who was I to deny her request?

She was my fated mate, though I would not lay that burden on her. I would wait until the show was over and the fear of discovery was gone. I would prove to her I was worthy of her love and when she gave her heart to me, I would share the symbol on my wrist. What was growing between us would not be denied.

But for now, I only wanted to focus on loving her body, showing my feelings rather than speaking them aloud.

Soon, I'd be licking her, driving her to the same fever she'd given me. Then I'd ride her until she screamed out my name. We wouldn't be the first to use the emollient to make things slippery. It could be used to lubricate everywhere, and it was completely edible.

It would still dry on our skin. The blower just made it easier to step out of the sanitizer and dress right away without our clothing sticking to us.

I lifted her off her feet, holding her slick body close, and stepped into my room, kicking the door closed as I exited.

I walked across the room and tumbled her onto the bed, following her down, pressing her into the soft surface. It was so easy to claim her mouth. Her fever matched mine, and she met me more than halfway.

It was even easier to glide my fingers across her eager flesh.

Her gasps and sighs turned to groans as I kissed down to her breasts and sucked a nipple into my mouth.

I glided my thumb along her crease, and she spread her legs wide.

"Like that, yes," I said, kissing across her belly. "I want to taste everything you have to offer."

27
WREN

I lay with my legs splayed wide on Throm's bed, a place where I never thought I'd find myself. A year ago, he'd brought me to a fever pitch, then left me. Now we'd finish what we'd started.

It didn't take long for his mouth on my breast and his fingers between my legs to drive me wild. I could barely think, but oh, how I could feel. The warmth of his body against mine, the heavy thrum of his heart beneath my fingertips, and the emotions pouring through me. I'd had sex, but never like this. I'd never felt a connection with someone else before.

I'd missed out on so much.

I bucked against his hand, wanting to feel his fingers or cock buried inside me. At this point, I didn't care which. I just had to succumb to my overwhelming need to feel our hearts surging together.

He exhaled, his breath making my skin quiver. Goosebumps ripped across my flesh, but I liked it. Craved it. The tingles sunk deeper when he sucked my clit into his mouth.

While I surged against him, he sucked and ran his

tongue across my clit. His big thumb dipped inside me. When he glided it in and out, the slow pace dragged the heat from deep inside me. It spread through my bones and made my heart race.

My mind started to soar through the roof, and my body quivered. He must've sensed I was about to fall apart.

He backed away, licking my essence off his lips, and shot me a heady smile.

"I want to take you from behind," he said.

I was more than open to that. I rose to my knees, presenting my ass his way. This tugged me back to that night an interstellar year ago, when I would've done anything to be with him. He'd touched a part of me no one else had, and I'd wanted more.

"I've dreamed about this view a thousand times and beat myself up for leaving you in this position." His hands grabbed my hips, holding tight. "Now I'm going to finish this. Give you everything I should've an interstellar year ago."

"Throm."

"What?"

"Stop talking and start doing."

He chuckled and centered his cock at my opening.

I pushed back when he surged forward. Oh, yeah, it felt amazing. I wanted to scream at him to fuck me. Was it bad that I liked dirty talk while in bed? I wasn't sure what he'd think about that, and now probably wasn't the time to ask him. But . . .

"Fuck me," I hissed.

"What?" He paused mid-stroke.

Damn, I'd shocked him. He was a sophisticated chef, so kind and sweet and polite all the time. He'd think I was smutty, and to a big extent, I was. I'd learned not to feel ashamed of that, though. I'd learned to embrace it. This was me, and I *liked* me. I wouldn't pretend to be anything but Wren.

"Do you like it hard, mate?" he growled, bending over me. "Do you want me to fuck you?" He was so much taller than me. There was no way he could nibble my neck while plunging his cock into me. But he somehow curled his upper body around so he could speak in my ear. Each word shot down my spine like an electric jolt.

"Yes, fuck me, Throm. Fast while you're at it too."

"I'm big."

"No shit. It feels amazing. I need to feel more of that big cock, Throm."

He chuckled, and the movement of his body blasted from his cock into me.

My groan rang out.

"You're incredibly tight," he said. "All I want to do is plunge my cock into you, over and over, but I don't want to hurt you. You're so much smaller than me everywhere."

"Try me."

"What?"

Sometimes, he could come across aloof His sophistication had impressed me from the moment I met him. But if we were going to make something work between us, he had to see me for who I was on the inside, not just the outside.

"I like it hard and gritty, and you're the only one who can give me what I need."

"Oh, yeah, I can," he said.

But he held my hips steady and continued to move within me in a slow rhythm that made my clit throb and flames roar through me. The primal part of me I covered up in public surged to the surface. This part of me wanted to beg him to claim me every way he could.

"Throm."

"Yes, mate?"

I loved that he called me that. It made me feel cher-ished. Special. As if I meant more to him than a casual fuck.

"Show me everything you've got."

He laughed again and began riding me hard and fast. Oh, yes, that was how I wanted it. Sometimes, slow and sweet could be incredible, but for this, our first time, I needed him to imprint himself on my skin to prove to me it had finally happened. He left me a year ago, and I'd spent too many nights dreaming of this. Softness just wouldn't do.

I savored each thrust, pressing my head into the blan-kets that smelled of him. The emollient made our bodies slippery, adding to the natural lubrication excreted by his cock. I'd noted that right away in the sanitizer. He had tiny nubs along his length and when I'd rubbed, they'd released slick fluid. What could be better than that?

Oh, I knew. Tasting it. That would come later.

I boiled inside, nearly surging through the roof. Each of his thrusts drove me closer to taking everything I needed. And from his groans, he was getting what he needed out of this too.

It was him. Me. Us. A blend of flesh and sweat and heat. Primal lust morphing into the beginnings of a lasting love.

He went faster, bracing my hips when his thrust would've shot my body away from his. I loved how tightly he held me, how he pumped in then pushed just a little bit farther to make sure I felt it all.

He curled his upper body again, placing his chin on my shoulder. His hand slid underneath me to find my clit, rubbing.

He carefully ran his claws across my inner thighs, and the scrape felt exquisite.

That was all it took. Him surrounding me. Him inside me. Him focusing me with his claws.

My body convulsed with a powerful orgasm.

He nibbled on my shoulder as he shot himself deep within my core.

28

THROM

"I have to go to my own room," she said from the shelter of my arms. "I want to stay with you all night and share myself with you again, but we can't take a chance we'll be caught."

Nothing would make me happier than to hold her—love her—all night, but I understood what she was saying.

We didn't dare risk this.

I teased my fingers up her spine, and she shivered. Her smile bloomed and she was the loveliest person I'd ever seen. My need for her was so much more than a physical thing. Only when I was with her—when I touched her—did I feel complete. She was my everything, and I refused to let her go.

"We're close. Omyn will be eliminated in the next round," I said.

"He's won twice. The odds are more in his favor." She braced herself on my chest and looked down at me. "If he's eliminated, we need to talk about what we'll do after that."

"You mean talk about what we'll do after this is over," I

said, my hands stilling. "And what we'll do on the show when it comes down to me and you."

"I'll compete," she said fiercely. "Never doubt that."

"I'll do the same." My voice reflected the sadness sucking away the wonderful moment we'd just shared. Neither of us would win if we competed against each other.

If she won, she'd be given her dream job and money to start a new life. I worried she'd see it as a failure to rise above her upbringing if she didn't come in first.

If I won, I could help my sister. I'd also have the chance to expand my brand, something I might never be able to do on my own. Losing meant finding a different way to pay for my sister's care. I was already strapped paying for the services she received. My career might not suffer, but it wouldn't grow in the way I'd always dreamed.

We'd both lose no matter what.

Could the relationship we were forming survive something like that?

"Maybe it won't come down to me versus you," she said, watching my face. Could she see the conflict brewing inside me? "Maybe Omyn will win, and we'll be sent home." Her eyes filled with shadows, and I hated that the mood between us had been broken. We'd shared something special. Preserving us was what truly mattered.

But sometimes a person couldn't control what life delivered.

"Let's see how the next event goes," I said. "We'll find a time to talk after that."

"Unless he kills me."

"That's not going to happen," I vowed. "I won't let him near you."

Biting her lower lip, she nodded.

She left, and I realized we'd talked about possible

outcomes based on who won the next event, but we hadn't gotten to us.

I lay awake a long time, thinking about how we could get through this together, but by the time I fell asleep early in the morning, I hadn't found an answer.

I woke sometime later, the soft vibration of the warp drives thrumming through my bones. Omyn must've boarded, and we were on our way to the next location.

Where would this ship take us, and what could we expect there? In this, I also had no answer.

I rose and stepped into the sanitizer, remembering how amazing it was to share this tiny space with Wren.

Worry about our future would mess with my mind. I needed to put that aside and focus on the show and keeping Wren safe.

Since Wren must be awake, I dressed and strode to the galley.

Only Omyn occupied the room. He sat at a table, delicately eating.

He nudged his head to the other side of the table. After making myself a cup of cavast in the synthesizer, I took the steaming mug to the table and sat across from him. Honestly, I'd rather be with Wren or alone, but there was no harm in sitting at the same table. Choosing a different one could be seen as an insult, and despite how he behaved, I wouldn't lower myself to his level.

"I had best time last night," he said with a sharp smile. "Too bad you miss out on prize."

There was no loss in how I'd spent my evening. Nothing could compare to being with Wren.

"Of course," he said. "If you win, I have to kill you."

It would be wise to ignore his taunt.

I'd never been very wise.

"You might try, perhaps," I said, sipping my cavast before lowering the cup carefully to the table. I kept my fingers looped through the handle.

"If I kill you here in galley, I make sure she not win even if she win," he said, his eyes flaring. "It be easy. She puny. Weak."

I lifted my cup and flung the scalding cavast at him, making sure it impacted with both his faces. He reeled back, upsetting his chair and toppling onto the floor. On the way down, he hit one of his heads hard against the wall. It lolled while the other remained alert. He glared at me with watery eyes and a face that had gone scarlet due to the burn. The color would fade quickly; the synthesizers never made anything too hot, but perhaps he'd learned a lesson.

I stood over him, prepared to smack him across the alert head if he so much as mentioned Wren again, but he remained on the floor and kept his mouth shut.

"If you touch her, you won't live long enough to share the details with the world." I pivoted and returned to the synthesizer, ordered two cups of cavast, then took them with me when I left the galley. I purposefully didn't look his way as I strode through the doorway.

I banged my elbow on Wren's door and she cracked it open.

A smiled filled her face as she swung the panel wide. "Oh, my god, cavast." She grabbed a cup from me and backed into her room. "Don't just stand there. Come on in."

"I planned to go to my room."

She shot a glare toward the hall. "All right. I'll see you later, chef?" Her voice lifted an octave, and her face lost that look of affection I was beginning to savor. It was for the best. Our stolen moment last night couldn't be repeated.

"Yes, later," I said casually, turning to stroll to my room.

Inside, I moved over to stand in front of the connecting door, hoping she'd open it from her side.

She didn't, but that was okay.

I'd bathed my heart in the warmth of her smile, and that would hold me for now.

29
WREN

The prince's ship landed at our next destination, the planet Kangora. We disembarked outfitted in new cooking tunics and pants and stood on sandy soil that stretched for hectains in all directions. Two suns sliced through the brilliant purple sky and sweat trickled down my spine.

Omyn wore a perpetual scowl, but what else was new? The location couldn't dampen his enthusiasm any further. He was determined to win this, and if that meant killing directly or with deceit, he'd be happy to do it. I'd stay out of his arm's reach as much as I could.

"Did they bring us to the wrong place?" I asked, sidling closer to Throm.

He shrugged and shielded his eyes, pointing. "What's that?"

I peered in that direction, seeing a few specks on the horizon. They grew bigger, morphing from dark spots into creatures almost as big as the ship we'd arrived in.

Three. And three of us.

I didn't like what I suspected.

Jell's pod landed in the sand and the top opened. He zipped out on his hover jet and soared over to float in front of us.

"Welcome, welcome!" he said, his eyes sparkling, and his face wreathed with a smile.

Camera bots hovered close enough to catch his every expression and if I guessed right, the quality of his pores.

The audience wouldn't be watching yet, but the camera bots would capture some great shots—of our dismay if that was available—and broadcast them as part of the warm-up to the next broadcast.

"As you can tell, we've brought you to Kangora," Jell said. "For today's event, you'll be asked to prepare a dessert." He smirked. "A dessert in the desert." Grinning, he waited for the canned applause that appeared on cue. His arm swept out to the dust churning through the air behind him. "I imagine you've noticed the lovely creatures pacing toward us."

"We going to cook them?" Omyn asked with a snicker.

When I sent a scowl his way, he huffed. "What you problem?" He frowned as he took in my closeness to Throm. "We cook what they give, beast itself, feces, or fur."

Please don't let us have to cook feces or fur. Or a live beast.

"Come now, Omyn," Jell said. "Kindness goes a long way."

This, from the host who encouraged us to fight it out when there was a tie?

When the creatures grew closer, metal bars glinted in the sunshine. The bars affixed to their collars connected them, making them move as one unit.

Platforms were mounted on their backs, and I spied cooking stations. Lovely.

"They're trixaks," Throm said. "A normally docile creature used to transport the people of this region across the desert."

"We'll cook standing on top of them," I said, already trying to imagine how I could take advantage of this. Until I knew the mystery ingredient, I wasn't sure what I'd prepare, but it would be sweet, and the presentation would be amazing. It had to be. While I hadn't come in last place in either of the first rounds, I hadn't won either. I'd wind up at the bottom if I didn't kick my game in gear.

"Mount one of them on the sides, and I'll grab a middle," he said softly.

I adored that he was so eager to protect me, but in doing so, he endangered himself.

"I can take the middle this time." I stepped forward, away from him. If we were seen close together too often, someone would put one and one together and blend us into a twosome. I couldn't risk myself and even more, I refused to risk him. He deserved to win as much as me.

I studied the placid, sand-colored creatures who slowed as they approached. Brown-skinned aliens rode on the trixak's necks, their legs splayed along the sides, as they controlled the pace of the beasts. The creature's long trunks swung back and forth, and their tails remained upright like a spike with a big, bushy pom-pom on the top. They periodically used it to swat insects buzzing around their faces.

They came to a stop and dropped forward, settling on the ground with their front legs splaying out beneath their trunks.

The riders hopped off and turned. They jogged out into the desert, and, in no time, they'd disappeared from view.

"Where are they going?" I asked, though I didn't direct my question to anyone in particular.

"We'll meet them on the opposite side of the plain," Jell said. "They'll judge your dishes."

"I assume we'll cook as the creatures cross the open area?" Throm asked.

"Indeed," Jell said. "You'll have the time it takes to cross the desert to prepare your dessert. The clock runs out when you reach a bright orange line on the opposite side."

"How long will that take?" I asked, looking for the trick. There was always one, and it would trip me up if I wasn't careful.

"Fifteen minues or so," Jell said.

I squinted, trying to sift through the heat waves shimmering across the desert to see our destination. "Won't it take longer than that?"

"Not at a full run," Jell said.

"We cook on running beast?" Even Omyn sounded shocked. His six arms shot up before settling at his sides. "How we do that?"

"Carefully," Jell said with a grin. "Very carefully."

"Who will control the beasts?" Throm asked, studying the cooking stations. I'd noted cabinets beneath that would contain the ingredients we'd sort through to find things to enhance our dish.

"They do not need to be controlled," Jell said. "Once you have taken a place on your station, we will turn them around, and they will find their way to the destination all on their own."

I bit back a sigh. I'd make this work. But, jeez, it would almost be nice to be cooking back at the restaurant. At least there, the grill didn't rock around, and I wouldn't be attacked if I prepared an excellent dish. With Madame Bellamay, it would be the opposite, her limbs smacking me if I didn't make something up to her sometimes odd standards.

"We start," Omyn said, rushing toward the center beast. Of course he'd try to separate us. Then, if one of us won, he'd be in the perfect position to attack.

Not having it. I ran forward and shouldered him away from the middle creature. He stumbled and his jaws dropped. He didn't think I had it in me, did he? Well, I'd show him.

Throm had the same idea as Omyn, though he wasn't rough about it. He started to nudge me toward the trixak on the far right.

"Not so fast, my chefs," Jell said, his voice threaded through with grating glee. "You must collect your mystery ingredient before you mount your beast."

"You deliver when we on board," Omyn said.

"No," Jell said kindly, though a sly smile lifted his thick lips. He waved to the right of the trixaks where something was bubbling out of the ground.

Soon, a large, inky black pool emerged. Bright orange balls bobbed around like eyeballs in a tristeen soup.

"Ulgri weed," Throm whispered. He grabbed my arm and half-dragged me toward the pool about twenty feet across. "Dive in and grab one."

"What's ulgri weed?" I asked.

"It's sweet. Like keevar."

Keevar tasted like what Earthlings used to call yogurt. Sweet yet tart.

"How do we prepare ulgri weed?" I asked, eager to hear any tips he might have to offer.

"Peel it and use the inner flesh." Throm tugged me closer. "Quickly. I have a feeling the beasts will take off whether we're all on their backs or not."

As we jumped into the pool, sinking into the black gook, Omyn roared. Without pause, he leapt in beside us, sending a black wave zipping toward the shore. When he emerged, the tar-like muck coated him, dripping down his two heads.

He held up an ulgri and started toward shore.

30
THROM

I grabbed an ulgri at the same time as Wren. We sloshed to shore and raced toward the enormous trixaks.

As Omyn approached the one on the far left, it lifted its snout. When he passed to approach the side of the beast, it shot a stream of liquid at him, knocking him from his feet. His ulgri popped from his grip and bounced across the ground. When he scrambled to his feet, taking off after the ulgri, his chef's outfit was now clean, though coated with sand.

"It's a trixak shower," I shouted to Wren. "Brace yourself."

I approached the trixak in the center but paused when its trunk lifted, squaring my feet in the sand. When the liquid hit, I held my breath and remained steady, only taking a step back from the impact. As soon as I had been cleansed by the creature, it allowed me to approach its side. A jump, and I landed on the cooking platform.

Wren did the same, stopping in front of the creature on the right. But when the liquid hit her, she was flung back onto her ass. She rose to her feet and shot me a grin.

Good. She wasn't hurt.

It didn't take her long to scramble up the side of the trixak and lower her ulgri onto the butcher block to the right of the grill.

She peered around. "How do we hold on?"

"You don't," I said. "Spread your legs and try to keep your knees loose. Roll with the pace of the beast."

The trixak rose to their feet and lumbered around to face the other direction. The subtle rocking motion made it easy to remain stable.

"Wait," Omyn cried, grabbing his ulgri from the ground and racing toward the remaining trixak. "I cook. I cook."

Once the trixak faced their destination, their big ears rose from where they'd laid across the sides of their heads, and their trunks pointed straight out.

Omyn jumped and grabbed onto the leg of his cooking station as the beasts burst into speed.

They bolted, and I soon adjusted to their rocking pace.

Dessert. I needed to stop watching Omyn struggle to climb his trixak and get working. I only had fifteen minues.

Wren had already stooped down in front of her cupboard and was pawing through the ingredients. She was an amazing chef. I'd seen how creative and unique her dishes were. She would not be easy to beat if it came down to us two.

I opened the cupboards and looked through the ingredients. While the ulgri might be sweet, the slightly bitter taste could ruin the dish. The flavor could be cut with herbs, but which would work best for a dessert? I'd only eaten ulgri once, and I'd never prepared it, but the dish I'd sampled had been a main course, not a sweet to follow.

I spied some remon seeds, which could be ground and would balance the bitter tang of the ulgri. I grabbed a handful and placed them in a small bowl, then added the other ingredients that would fit with the dish I was dreaming up. It was a bolder offering than I might normally choose, but where else could I try something like this? The judges lived here; they enjoyed these ingredients. If I could craft something that was both unique and new, plus familiar because everything came from this planet, I could win this.

I straightened and placed the bowl on my food prep surface, noting Omyn had made it to the top and was clawing his way across the platform, aiming for his cooking station. He'd lost a few minues, but I was confident he'd soon catch up. I didn't doubt his chef abilities for even one secunda.

Wren was chopping her ulgri, confidently removing the outer skin and exclaiming about the bright pink flesh on the inside.

"The seeds . . .?"

"Cannot be eaten," I said.

"Cheating," Omyn cried, pointing at us. "They cheating."

Jell followed us, coasting along on his hover jet, staying clear of the flicking bushy tails of the racing trixaks.

"Chefs are allowed to help each other," I said. "Remember?"

Omyn grumbled, but he could either keep arguing or he could make a dessert. His eagerness to win beat his urge to squabble.

The beasts didn't appear concerned to have us on their backs, so I focused on my task, making quick work of cleaning my ulgri. I filleted it thin and set the pieces aside to rest, then began to make a creamy sweet sauce with a few of the other ingredients.

Wren had placed her ulgri in a microblender and was pulsing it while swaying her hips. What an excellent idea. After she's pureed other ingredients with the ulgri, she poured it into a chill-maker that would turn it into a creamy slush within minues.

She dropped three bowls onto her counter then placed a frying pan on her heat conductor, turning the burner on beneath.

I left her to her task, needing to work on my own dishes before it was too late.

In no time, we reached the edge of the desert where a covered platform had been set up. Our three judges sat on cushions in the center of the platform, studying us as our beasts approached.

When we were only a short distance from the platform, the trixaks came to a halt. They dropped to their knees and then their bellies with heavy sighs.

I held onto my dishes as the cooking station rocked with the motion.

Wren grinned my way, sharing a mutual concern for what would come next. No matter what, we were in this together.

"Your time is . . . up," Jell shouted. "Your dishes will be transported by hover beam to our lovely judges who will soon decide who has won this round!"

Misty beams erupted overhead and shot down to engulf our dishes. Lifted up into the beams, one plate from each of us was then placed in front of the judges.

One sighed and released a bright smile, bobbing his head toward us. "Good. Good."

I hoped he was looking at my dish or Wren's. It was time to knock Omyn out of the game.

"Cheaters," Omyn hissed. "Remember what I say in galley," he snarled at me.

I lifted my brows. "I think you're the one with a short attention span. Remember what *I* said in the galley?"

He flexed his six fists and before the judges had a chance to take even one bite, Omyn leapt in my direction.

He hit me in the gut, and we toppled over the side of my trixak.

31
WREN

Throm and Omyn slammed onto the sand between my trixak and Throm's.

The creatures shrieked and lumbered to their feet. They stomped and spun as one unit, barely missing crushing Omyn and Throm. The guys swung fists, impacting flesh, and released grunts as they scrambled across the ground.

"Ah, a fight," Jell said, zipping over to hover beside me. "Would you like to bet on who will win the battle?"

I reeled on him. "Are you kidding me?"

His lips soured. "No need to be like that."

Camera bots surrounded the two males to take in the action from all angles.

They sprang to their feet.

Omyn slashed out with two of his six claws.

I bit my nails, trying to find a way off this stupid trixak. I needed to do something to help Throm.

Throm sucked in his belly and backed up a pace, putting himself almost beneath the middle trixak. The beast roared, its trunk swinging in Throm's direction, and the beast scrambled sideways. This tugged my trixak along with it since they were still attached to one another.

Throm dove forward, rolling and coming up in front of Omyn. A kick sent Omyn flying beneath my trixak's feet.

I clung to the platform as my trixak bellowed and smacked Omyn with its tail, sending the Sevest male skidding across the sand.

Throm stomped after him, grabbing Omyn at the back where his two necks connected to his torso. Holding him out at arm's length, he shook Omyn while the other male flailed, his feet dangling. He tried to swipe out at Throm, but his arms weren't long enough to reach.

His legs rose, and he thrust them at Throm, hitting him hard in the belly. Throm stumbled backward and fell, tossing Omyn to the side.

With my heart in my throat, I leaned over the edge of my platform to watch.

My trixak shifted its hips, and I fell forward. I landed hard on my back in the sand, the wind knocked from my lungs. Dazed, I shook my head before realizing the grunts I heard came from Omyn and Throm still fighting nearby.

I rolled onto my belly and rose to my hands and knees. Realizing I was beneath the belly of a trixak, I crawled forward before it could trample me. Beyond the trixak, I stood and peered around.

Omyn had Throm pinned to the ground, holding him with four arms while the other two clawed Throm's chest.

I grabbed a rock and raced around the trixaks while Throm bucked. But he couldn't shake Omyn.

I crept between two of the creatures, approaching Omyn from behind.

Throm cried out in pain and kicked Omyn, who fell to

the side. Throm got to his feet and staggered toward Omyn lying on the ground.

I rushed forward, passing Throm who had blood pouring down his chest. His dazed gaze connected with me, and he groaned. I threw the rock, and it hit Omyn in the side of his right head. The eyes rolled back while the others fixed on me. Omyn got to his feet with a snarl and scrambled toward me, his claws lifted.

Throm smacked Omyn's other head as he passed, making the Sevest warrior stagger backward. He twirled around before tangling in his feet and toppling to the ground like a felled tree.

I grabbed another rock and stomped toward him, but Throm caught me around the waist and tugged me back into his arms.

"It is all right," he said softly by my ear. "He won't be rising soon."

My breathing raged in and out of me while the trixaks shifted and bellowed. But with the fight over, they settled, dropping back onto their bellies to rest.

"Ah, now that was entertaining," Jell said, flying in close behind us. "Thank you both for providing such a stimulating break while the judges sampled your dishes."

I broke free of Throm's arms and rushed toward Jell, slamming my head into his belly. He shot backward, groaning. "Why did you do that?"

"Stay away from us." I put my hands on my hips and glared. "Or the next time, I'll aim lower."

32
THROM

Before she did more damage, I grabbed Wren's hand and tugged her away from Jell. I wanted to hold her, but the damn camera bots were close enough they'd pick up every crease on our faces.

"That was brave," I said. Not necessarily wise, but I admired her for acting rather than snarling. It was no different than what I'd done with Omyn.

Speaking of the Sevest warrior, he still lay on the ground. While I'd be happy to see him trampled by the trixaks, I wasn't going to win by cheating.

I made sure Wren was okay—she stared at Jell and growled, but she didn't appear poised to attack him again. Scooting between the trixaks, I grabbed Omyn's feet and dragged him away from the creatures.

He groaned and shifted, and I was confident he'd wake up soon, as surly as he'd been before. He'd bear watching, but perhaps he'd learned a bit of caution. The next time he attacked; however, he wouldn't give warning.

I joined Wren just in time to hear Jell speak to her in a

low voice. "I'm warning you. Don't do anything like that again or else."

Great. More threats.

I shot him a glare. "You'll have to get through me first."

Jell huffed, but his face lost half its color. Taking on a small female was different than challenging a large male. "Behave. I'm watching you."

He soared up over the trixaks, swatting away camera bots that got too close. See? It wasn't enjoyable being scrutinized all the time.

Wren and I strode around the trixaks to stand in front, though out of trunk's reach.

The judges still sampled our food, releasing low grunts and mumbles that could mean almost anything.

Finally, they looked to each other and nodded.

Jell flew down close to them before turning to face us.

"We have a winner and a loser," he cried. His cheery mood appeared restored except for the hatred lingering in his eyes when he looked my way. I could live with it. I'd rather he direct his anger toward me than Wren.

Omyn staggered out from behind the trixaks to join us, though he stood at least three arm's lengths away from me. He didn't look my way, and he didn't say a thing.

"The winner of this round is Wren," Jell shouted. His glare slid from me to her, and I realized I hadn't done anything to diminish his hatred toward her; he'd expanded it to include me. We not only had to watch out for Omyn, but we'd also made an enemy of our host.

Jell floated closer to Wren, though he kept his distance for safety. "The judges only had praise for your dish. Such a creative way to use the ulgri weed." He might be saying the right things, but there was no mistaking the anger heightening his color. "And your sauce was exquisite."

"I won?" Wren asked, giddy. She deserved this victory. I'd seen her dish and had been solidly impressed.

"Congratulations," I said, shooting her a grin.

"Thanks," Wren said, looking toward Omyn. "Maybe my prize will be a solid night's sleep without fear of being attacked."

Jell did a quick backflip before hovering in front of us. "And the loser of this match is . . ."

Drumbeats rang out, followed by gasps from the pretend audience.

"The loser is Omyn," Jell cried.

The camera bots zipped over to Omyn to capture his expression. He stiffened and snarled at us. "You think you win?" His arms shot up over his head. "They fraternize. Fraternize!"

"What are you talking about?" Jell asked. "Surely you're not suggesting that Thrombuka and Wren have become more than friends."

"Fraternize. I see," Omyn cried. "Cameras see."

There were none present last night. Wren wasn't the only one who'd made sure of that before we shared our first kiss.

Would Jell use this chance to get even? If he accused us, it would be our word against his, and he was the host of the show. They needed him more than us. Wren and I would be booted from the show, creating lots of drama for the viewers, and Omyn would be elevated to supreme winner by default.

"You together," Omyn shouted. His thigh muscles bunched, and he formed fists at his sizes.

"Do you have evidence, Omyn?" Jell asked. He watched us, but we wouldn't do anything to make him suspect there was some truth in Omyn's statement.

"Fraternization!" With a mighty roar, Omyn ran toward us.

I stepped between him and Wren, but before he could reach us, a trixak trunk snapped out and encircled his waist. He was lifted up over the trixak's head. The trunk snapped back and forth, whipping Omyn in multiple directions.

Squirming, Omyn cried out, his snarl of dismay turning to a yelp of pain. He beat at the trunk, his claws digging deeply.

Wren dragged her gaze away, focusing on the sand, and I did the same. Whatever happened to Omyn couldn't be halted now. I wasn't strong enough to challenge the trixak.

The trixak tossed Omyn up into the air, releasing him, but when Omyn fell toward the ground, another trixak grabbed him and did the same. They played with him like they would a ball.

Jell watched what happened with pure bliss on his face.

Omyn released another cry.

"Halt," Jell shouted. "Enough. Release him. It's time for him to return to his home planet in defeat."

The trixak dropped Omyn, and he staggered. Two droids zipped in and grabbed his arms, leading him toward a shuttle parked partway out into the desert.

Wren gulped, and I wanted to hold her, to tell her things would work out all right. That this was just part of the show, and Omyn wasn't more than shaken up. But any indication we were more with friends would be met with questions from Jell.

Omyn had accused us, but it didn't appear Jell was taking the bait.

The trixaks stopped shifting, though they watched Omyn intently until the droids had helped him into a small shuttle. The craft lifted off the ground, taking Omyn to an orbiting ship that would return him to his home planet.

After stepping off the platform, the judges approached the trixaks. They mounted the beast's necks and turned them toward the desert. The creatures broke into a trot that turned into a rolling gallop, and the trixaks soon disappeared from view.

Jell waved the camera bots and soared in close to me and Wren. "If there is any truth in Omyn's statement, I will discover it. You know what we do with those who break the rules."

We said nothing, just stared forward blankly. Denying it would be a lie, but unless they gave us truth serum, we wouldn't admit something happened.

Eventually, Jell huffed. "Omyn is one of the lucky ones," he said blandly. He looked to the camera bots who'd returned to float nearby. "We can be generous. Magnanimous. And we don't wish anyone harm. Omyn was sent back to his home planet. In defeat, but almost as safe as he was when he arrived. This is just another part of Interstellar Chef, am I right?" His lips twitched upward before he smoothed them. "I cannot wait for the next event, can you, Throm?" His words might be directed at me, but he watched Wren with an evil light in his eyes.

He hadn't sought revenge for her actions; he was just waiting for the right opportunity to act.

For the first time—and I'd watched this show a lot in the past—I realized who most enjoyed the dangerous side of the events.

Jell.

And the glare he shot us said he'd already decided that neither of us would finish this show alive.

33
WREN

Jell soared near and lifted my arm like I was a staggering prize fighter who'd barely survived a match. "Your prize for winning this event is—"

"I don't want it," I said. Frankly, I felt like rushing behind the judge's platform and throwing up. I hadn't liked Omyn. I knew he'd kill me given half a chance. But what had just happened to him made my belly churn. Sure, he'd survived, but he'd been toyed with. Tossed around like a sack of kartoffs. They'd wanted him to think he'd die.

This was supposed to be a fun cooking show. I guess. I knew in advance there could be danger, but I'd thought the cooking and *friendly* competition would be the focus, not torturing those who'd lost.

The fake cheers of the audience cut off, leaving only silence and the whir of the camera bots flying around us. Had the vid taken a sponsor break?

"What do you mean you don't want your prize?" Jell asked.

This confirmed my suspicion that they wanted enthusiasm from me, not a refusal. They'd start the camera bots again when I was willing to gush, which wasn't happening.

"You haven't heard what it is yet," he said. "Come, come. You'll enjoy this." His sly grin widened. "I promise."

Sure. Like I'd believe that?

"Donate it to someone needy," I said. "I don't want anything for the win."

"Well." Jell's face scrunched, and it was clear I'd offended him. Probably the producers too. I was already on his bad list for head butting Jell. Now I'd refused his moment to be the benefactor of what he must consider an exciting prize.

"Can Throm join me for whatever the prize is?" I asked.

He dropped his voice. "Don't think I'm not watching you two."

Yeah, but he hadn't seen anything yet. We'd made sure of that. We walked a very thin line, but as far as the multi-universe knew, we hadn't stepped off on either side.

"You won," Jell said. "The prize is for you."

"I'll share it, or I'll remain on the prince's ship tonight. I'm sure the viewers would find following me around the ship boring." I turned to Throm. "Do you play cards? I think we should play cards tonight. Like, Go Fish. Have you heard of that game? I've got a deck of cards we can use, and I'll outline the rules."

"Are fish involved?" Throm asked with a twinkle in his eyes.

"Nope. That would be too exciting. We'll play nice and slow, and we'll drink water. No alcohol so we don't start acting silly."

"We wouldn't want to act silly," Throm said.

"All right," Jell shouted. He waved for the camera bots to start filming again. "It appears we have an interesting proposal from our lovely winner, Wren. She has offered to share her prize with her fellow contestant, Thrombuka." He flashed a smile at the closest camera. "We at Interstellar Chef love a twist, and this one tops the cake. One could even suggest you both won since neither of you lost."

"Great," I said with a grin that made Jell's smile widen. I was a good girl. He would hold off killing me for now. "What's the prize?" I rubbed my palms together and hopped around like I was overjoyed. "I can't wait to hear. How about you, Throm?"

"I'm thrilled," he said blandly.

My laugh snorted out, but I covered the sound with my palm and widened my eyes for added measure. Mustn't make Jell any angrier.

"Your prize is . . ." Jell did a little dance to draw out the suspense while the audience's cheers grew louder. He cut them off with a slash of his hand. "A night in a desert pomgrole."

"What's a pomgrole?" I asked Throm.

"You're going to love it." From the eagerness of his eyes, I had a feeling he was already cooking up a plan that would allow us to both enjoy this pomgrole to its fullest extent.

After witnessing what happened to Omyn, the idea of celebrating made my spine twitch. I felt like hunkering down in a small hole in the ground and waiting until it was time to compete again. At least there, I'd be safe.

I'd worked hard to craft the best dish, but the win felt hollow.

"Hover jets will take you to the pomgrole," Jell said. "I believe you will thoroughly enjoy this prize donated by our wonderful sponsor, TigarsRUs, the premier distributor of exclusive spices from throughout the multi-universe. TigarsRUs. We spice up your life."

With a whirl, he turned away from me and flew up over us, circling us like a carrion bird. The camera bots followed, I assumed to showcase him with panoramic vids of the vast desert behind him.

Jell pressed a grin onto his face and stared at the closest camera bot. "Join us for the last round of this season's Interstellar Chef tomorrow, everyone. A new world, a new mystery ingredient, and a chance to see how this season finishes. Who will win the chance to cater the prince's wedding, plus a generous monetary prize? Who will be crowned the best chef of them all? Will Thrombuka trounce Wren in the finale, or will the stealthy female chef show him who's boss? Tune in then for the grand finale of . . . Interstellar Chef!"

His smile fell as fast as the camera bots winked out. He flew toward us on his hover jet, fury plastered on his face.

He skidded to a stop just shy of hitting me. "You will pay for what you did and your uncooperative attitude."

"You don't enjoy surprises in the show?" I asked, savoring mocking him, though I shouldn't. If I were wise, I'd beg his forgiveness, not give him the verbal middle finger. "I thought the audience savored a dish full of heat?"

"Was Omyn right?" he sputtered. "Have you and Thrombuka been fraternizing?"

Such a formal term for hooking up. It was so much more than that between me and Throm.

I refused to give Jell the chance to use our feelings to hurt us.

"We're friends," I said. No lie there.

"Friends," Throm echoed.

I truly felt we should be together, and I'd tell the world as soon as we wouldn't be penalized for sharing.

Sometimes, love meant sacrificing everything if it meant you could be together.

"We're not doing anything we shouldn't," I added for good measure. Also not a complete lie.

"See that you don't," Jell said. "I stopped the trixaks from killing Omyn. This shows I can be kind and generous with anyone on the show. But you two . . . You know what will happen if I find out you've been secretly fraternizing." He spun and flew to his shuttle. After settling inside, the ship took him toward his craft waiting in orbit.

The camera bots flew into the box and a droid took them to a second waiting ship. They'd deploy again tomorrow for the final round of the show.

Frankly, I just wanted to lay on my bed on the prince's ship, preferably with Throm's arms around me, but we had a prize to claim.

How were we going to sneak some alone time tonight? The camera bots had been shut off, but that didn't mean someone wasn't watching. The warning in Jell's eyes would haunt me tonight.

"Where are the hover jets that are supposed to take us to the pomgrole?" I asked, peering around. Might as well get this over with.

No ships waited with open hatches, and I was just as happy the trixak hadn't returned.

"There they are," Throm said, pointing.

Hover jets soared near and dropped onto the ground in front of us. We stepped on them, and they fused to our feet and legs.

They took off and soared to our right, aiming for a long series of hills in the distance.

34
THROM

The hover jets coasted over the low hills, scaling higher until crisp, cool air surrounded us. I didn't know much about this planet, so I wasn't sure where we were going. I'd heard of pomgroles, which were a type of garden with lush vegetation and pools. I bet Wren was going to enjoy this prize.

We landed near the top of a large mountain, the hover jets touching down and buzzing for us to get off.

When we stood on the scruffy grass, Wren peered around. "Where to next?"

A light, floral scent reached me, and I pointed toward the center of the mountain that had been scooped out ages ago by some sort of natural phenomenon.

We took a path that was soon overgrown with lush, flowering vines arching over where we walked. I couldn't see far ahead, but I sensed we were heading in the right direction.

When we rounded a bend in the path, we stopped.

Wren gasped. "Wow. I'm impressed. I grew up on a space station. You know how much room that gives everyone but the wealthy. My mom and I shared an eight-by-eight room with two bedrooms that only fit the beds, plus a tiny synthesizer and a ratty couch in the main room. I couldn't roll over in my bed without hitting my elbows on the wall or smacking my head on the door. And let me tell you; when she brought a guy home . . ." She looked up at me and grinned, a totally unexpected gesture after her comment. "Here I go, talking about my childhood when instead, I could be enjoying this with you."

She raced forward, and I followed, grinning as she squealed and skipped around the edges of one steaming pool after another. On the opposite side of the small valley, she stopped beneath a series of falls, gazing up.

When she turned back to me, she sent me a coy smile. "Would swimming in my underwear be considered fraternizing? 'Cause I'm going to do it."

She yanked her tunic off and shimmied out of her pants, tossing them aside. Then she leaped into the closest pool, generating a big splash.

I jogged around the pools to stop beside the one she swam in. Her head bobbed up, and she turned my way.

"Come on in," she said, her sultry voice making fire flash through my veins.

"If I do," I said in a low, husky voice. "We'll definitely be fraternizing."

"Wouldn't want to upset Jell."

My humor fled because, despite her joke, she was right. If Jell or anyone found out we were together, they'd not only kick us off the show, but our lives may also be forfeit.

I nudged my head to the pool next to hers. "I'll take that one instead."

She nodded slowly. "I get it." Lying on her back, she

floated. Her bra-covered breasts bobbed above the water, and I was male enough to appreciate the view.

My cock twitched, reminding me of the joy I'd found in her body.

I stripped and stepped into the pool, sinking down until only my head remained above the surface.

"You're not wearing undies," she said, her eyes sparkling as she looked my way.

"You weren't supposed to look."

"I'd have to be dead not to look."

Another joke, but it dropped my belly all the way to the center of the planet. My heart too.

What was I going to do with this female? I ached to claim her, to show her off to the world. I didn't like hiding how I felt for her.

"I'm sorry," she said softly. "I didn't mean that. Well, I actually did, but I shouldn't have mentioned death."

"No problem. I feel the same."

Even speaking thoughts like this could be dangerous, though. A scan with my app indicated no camera bots nearby, but I couldn't take chances.

I floated on my back, and now she must have an interesting view, since my cock jutted up out of the water. I rolled and swam briskly across the big pool in the direction of the falls.

Wren climbed out of her pool and followed on foot, passing me when I stopped just out of reach of the plunging water.

"Lovely," she shouted, her voice barely cutting through the enormous splash. She moved around to the side to take in a different view before gingerly stepping forward.

In a moment, she was hidden from view.

35
WREN

"Cool," I said, and my voice echoed back at me. The falls plunged down into the pool on my left and on my right, I spied a cave. "Just like I've read about in books." A buried treasure. Pirates. Dashing, sword-wielding heroes.

Throm was my dashing hero.

He came up behind me and placed his hand on my lower back, caressing me while leaning close to speak into my ear. "Where do you think the cave leads?"

"I believe we should find out."

He was completely naked, and it was all I could do not to turn and leap into his arms. I wanted to feel that connection I'd found only with him. My heart craved the feel of him moving within me, the way his eyes lit up when he looked my way, and the sweet things he said.

My knees shaky from overwhelming emotions, I strode forward. He kept pace behind me, his fingers teasing down my spine.

While camera bots might hover outside, I didn't believe any would pass through the fine spray to keep up with us.

Feeling more confident, I continued to the mouth of the cave and peered inside.

"It's dark in there," I said. "Spooky."

"Then let's return to the pools," he said. "We don't want to encounter anything dangerous."

"I want to explore." I stepped inside and gave my eyes time to adjust. Soft dirt covered the cave floor, and I continued inward, taking in the glossy black stone covering the walls and roof. The cave sloped slowly downward, and I kept going, spying a dim light ahead.

Throm came with me, peering around, as curious as me to see what we might find.

We continued down a long hill until it bottomed out on a smooth surface. A series of connecting pools covered the floor of the large, three-story cave with huge stalactites jutting down from the ceiling. Some came close to touch the surface of the pools. Steam rose off the water, and I dipped a toe in.

"Too hot?" Throm asked.

"Just right." I focused on the smooth, murky water. "Do you think anything dangerous lurks in there?"

"There's only one way to find out." He jumped in, creating a splash that soaked me.

I sputtered but grinned as his head bobbed above the surface. "Care to fraternize with me?"

I gulped and looked around. "Can we trust we're alone?"

"Never, but I think we're safe enough swimming together, don't you?"

If I got close to him, we'd be doing a lot more than swimming.

And I wanted to get close. It felt like forever since we were together, though it was only the night before.

I couldn't see the bottom of the pool, however, which meant cameras wouldn't be able to either.

"Coming in," I shouted, my voice echoing as I dove into the big pool.

Remaining beneath the water, I swam toward him, discovering the murkiness was actually vegetation, and it only coated the surface. Below, it was as clear as day.

Before I ran into him, I placed my hands on his hips and glided them up his torso, keeping them below the water as my head popped up. I sucked in air and shot him a sly smile as I teased my fingers across his chest.

"Shall we play cards?" I asked. "Or would a word game be better? We're just casual friends, hanging out together in the water, so there's no harm in that."

He stifled a groan. "You're dangerous, woman."

"Ah, yes, a word game, then. Let me guess the movie you're naming. Stealing Fame?"

"That's it." His eyelids hooded as I brought my foot up to tease along his inner thigh.

Two could play the game within a game. His claws slid along my belly until his hand dipped beneath the band at the top of my panties. His other hand teased across the underside of my breast, nudging the fabric up until he could capture my nipple.

It was all I could do not to moan as his thumb stroked my clit.

"He's on fire," I said.

Throm frowned before his face cleared. "Flames be Mine."

"Mine too," I whispered, but I nodded to show he'd guessed correctly.

Was anyone watching? I couldn't tell, and at this point,

I didn't care. As long as I could keep from shrieking when I came, this would work.

I laid back on the surface, though I kept my lower body far enough down no one could see that Throm was driving me to the brink of the best orgasm of my life.

A fusion of hearts was building between us. It was a starship spiraling out of control. A meteor shooting across the sky. I closed my eyes, drinking in the feel of him, his warmth and power. How gentle he was with me, using his claws with just enough pressure to make me ache, but never enough to cause harm.

I was too short compared to him to reach his cock, but that didn't slow him down. He carefully turned me and left my breast long enough to point upward. "What does that stalactite remind you of?"

His thick, long cock, but I had a feeling naming that wasn't part of our game.

"A rocket," I said. A hiss of pleasure escaped my throat as he eased my underwear to the side and pushed his cock inside me.

The water sloshed a bit as he pulled out and drove himself forward.

"And that one?" he asked, pointing again.

He wanted me to think? All I could do was feel the slow thrust of him burying himself over and over. I felt like I stood on the tip of a spire. I'd fall, but Throm would be there at the bottom to catch me.

I wanted to cling and groan, to tell him how much he meant to me, but I had to act like we were casually floating around in the pool.

His fingers found their way to my clit while he pointed to one stalactite after another, naming what they looked like himself. He must've seen I was too far gone, too close to play this game any longer.

I floated, acting as if I was examining the water. Keeping my head curved down helped hide my expression. Bliss must've consumed my face.

I couldn't do it. I was tumbling down a hillside, unable to stop my momentum. I'd shriek my lungs out when the powerful orgasm hit me. But I had to hold on, had to bite down hard on my lip to keep all but a whimper from slipping out.

He shifted his hips, burying himself inside me over and over.

"She's on a pulmar roof," I whispered.

"What?" he asked, pausing.

"You won't find the answer unless you try *harder*," I half-growled.

He chuckled and started moving again. His fingers rolled my clit, and I literally saw the roar of the explosion coming for me. It blasted across my body, and shockwaves followed. A soft gasp escaped my lips.

Throm held my hips and pushed himself deeper, giving me everything he had and more until I felt him shudder within me.

I sagged; grateful Throm held me afloat. My eyes remained closed, and I panted, savoring the ripples echoing through me, centering at the connection he'd just forged between us.

"Game, Set, Point," Throm said, with deep satisfaction riding his voice.

He pulled out of me and straightened my clothing with infinite care. After, he casually swam toward one of the stalactites. "This one looks like a pole, don't you think?"

I watched him. Loved him. There was no denying it

now. Each time we came together, our bond grew stronger. Nothing and no one was going to tear us apart.

"It does, Throm." I jerked my head toward the slope we'd descended to get here. The big question was: would my trembling body support me if I tried to walk? "Do you think they left any food on the surface? All this . . . swimming has worked up my appetite."

"I imagine they did," he said, a smile trembling across his lips. The look he gave me . . . I made my breath catch. Joy was a powerful thing, and he handed it to me with each grin. "I believe we'll find you something that will satisfy."

36
THROM

After we located a pack with food and beverages, we sat on a grassy area and ate until we were ready to burst.

I kept remembering the wonder of being with Wren deep within the cave. Her soft gasps, the warmth I found in her eyes. I hoped it meant she longed to be with me always, because I wasn't sure how I'd go on without her. We'd talk soon, and I'd bare my very soul to her. Would she turn me away?

We remained in or around the pools all night, finding ways to sneak in as much pleasure as possible.

I took her beneath the falls where no camera bot could see, and she sucked me off when we'd parted to find bushes as if for relief, only to sneak into the dark shadows beneath an enormous boulder.

By morning, we slept, though not in each other's arms like we both wanted. In case anyone watched, we kept a decent amount of distance between us.

Just like friends would do.

The hover jets arrived in the morning to retrieve us, and

we dressed quickly in the clean clothing they brought with them.

We were taken to the prince's ship, and we boarded the craft.

Jell had yet to make an appearance, but I assumed we'd see him soon. He wouldn't miss a chance to taunt us.

Tired from not much sleep, I dropped on my bed and was out for horus, only waking when Wren tapped on the connecting door.

"Hey, I think we're landing soon."

Yes, the last day of the show. The last event.

I noted the change in the sound of the engines.

"Thanks." Rising, I stood in the sanitizer, then donned the last official chef's tunic and pants.

Today, Wren and I would compete with each other. Only one of us would win, and my heart was going to ache no matter what the outcome.

I wanted her to get her chance at a new, better life, but my sister needed me. No, she had me already. I was with her when she took her first step alone, and I'd be there when she could finally run. But to get there, she needed money. Everything cost so much. I did well with my restaurant, but after paying her bills, I barely squeaked by.

When Wren and I met in the hallway outside our rooms, our gazes connected. I saw the same mix of excitement and sorrow there, and I didn't know what to think of it. Would she tell me tonight it was over? Or would she hold out her hand and tell me she wanted forever?

She nodded slowly. "I want everything wonderful for you today, Throm. May the best chef win."

The ship landed, and the hatch opened. Sunshine and numerous trees met us when we stepped down the ramp and onto the ground. While we looked around, waiting for Jell, the pilot joined us.

"Hey," Dekrin said. "Jell sent a message. He's been delayed, but he asked me to tell you to hike through the forest to the other side. He'll meet you there."

"How far of a walk is it?" Wren asked.

The pilot shrugged. "From the air, it looked like a hectist or so."

A two-hour walk then.

"Why not fly us there?" I asked, scratching the back of my neck. Something about this made me uneasy, but I couldn't quite pin down what it could be.

"You know, that's a great idea," the pilot said. "And I asked Jell about that, but he specifically instructed me to bring you here." He frowned in the direction of the woods. "I was assured this was safe, and it damn well better be."

I wasn't sure what the pilot could do if it wasn't.

"We could take hover jets," Wren said.

"The hovers that flew you in from your overnight excursion were claimed by Jell. He said they needed to charge," Dekrin said, and I only read honesty in his eyes. He scratched the back of his neck and swatted at a fleener darting around his head. "If you'd rather wait here, I'm sure Jell will come get you before the event."

"The show's about to start, though, right?" I asked.

Dekrin nodded, his lips thinning. "Tell you what. Let me go inside and call him. I don't like this, and I'm not putting anyone in an uncomfortable situation."

Wren held him back when he started to turn. "It's okay." She shot me a smile. "We don't mind a little walk in the woods, right?"

"It'll be fine," I finally said.

"I'll see you after the event, then." Dekrin's gaze shifted

between us. "I want to be there for the finish. You two have prepared some amazing dishes. You both deserve to win."

"Thanks," Wren said, her cheeks going pink.

A com hail rang out inside the craft, and Dekrin paused. "I guess I'd better go see what that's about." He strode inside the craft and soon returned to the open hatch, bracing his arms on the sides of the opening. "Something's come up, and I've been asked to pick up a few items on Jell's ship." His lips thinned, and his voice lowered. I wasn't sure he intended for us to hear. "Never thought I'd turn into a messenger yarling." With a shake of his head, he disappeared inside again. The hatch closed, and the ship lifted off the ground and soared up into the sky.

With a shared shrug, we started walking down a wide path that appeared to cut through the middle of the forest. Large birds swooped over the path periodically, but they remained high enough overhead, I wasn't concerned. A crick-crick-crick echoed from our right, and I wondered what kind of creature made the sound.

"Hot," Wren said, smacking a bug that had landed on her arm. She wiped her brow with her palm. "I hope there are drinks waiting for us on the other side of the forest. A donut would be nice too."

"I have a wonderful recipe for brunswell donuts I'll be happy to share."

"What do they taste like?" When she scrunched her face up like that, I found her incredibly cute. I'd long since given up fighting this. I was in love with her, and I'd feel this way for the rest of my life.

"They taste like Earth's version of heaven."

"I'm not sure that has a taste. But if they're anything like—"

A shriek rang out in the forest.

Wren froze and swallowed, staring around wildly.

The dull thuds of something big moving in our direction echoed around us.

Wren backed up until she ran into a tree. "What . . .?"

"I think Jell has found a way to get revenge," I said in a low voice.

Her eyes widened with horror.

I took her hand and bolted back in the direction we'd come from.

37
WREN

If Jell was here, I'd head-butt him again. He'd set us up, making us walk through a forest full of big creatures. Predators? We weren't hanging around to find out.

We reached the edge of the forest and raced across a wide open, stony area made up of big slabs of rock. The going was rough, and it was all uphill. My light sweat soon turned into streams jerking down my face and spine.

But the creature that chased us in the forest didn't leave the trees. As blue as the leaves around it, it stomped within the shade, snarling and gnashing its long tusks.

A shadow passed overhead, followed by another. Rather than look up, I grabbed a stick lying on the ground and hefted it.

Something cawed above us, and the shadow dipped our way.

Throm leapt on me, bringing me to the ground with a smack that jarred through my bones. He rolled, coming to a stop against a big boulder with me in his arms.

A bird the size of an escape pod with blue and white striped feathers swooped above us in circles, cawing.

It dove toward us, its white beak open and its neck extended. Claws scraped across the boulder above us while Throm rolled, taking us away from the base.

He jumped to his feet and hauled me up to stand beside him before I could do so myself. We ran.

The bird came after us, flying at our height. It was big enough to grab each of us in a claw and lift off. It would take us to its nest and devour us.

We crested the rocky hill and raced down the other side. A long plain made up of wavering grasses stretched ahead of us, and in the distance, something metal winked in the sunlight.

"There," I said, pointing. I wasn't sure what it was, but metal could mean civilization and safety.

"Can you keep going?" Throm yelled as we hit the plain and blasted across it, trampling the grass as we wove back and forth to make it harder for the bird to grab us.

"No choice."

When the whoosh of feathers roared toward me, I flung myself to the ground and rolled to the right, finding shelter within the deep grass.

The bird landed and peered around.

I froze, not even daring to blink.

I wasn't sure where Throm was, but I hoped he'd remain still until the bird gave up and took off.

The bird clawed at the ground and started striding in widening circles.

It sought us!

When its back was turned, I scrambled onto my hands and knees and crawled in the opposite direction, wiggling through a tunnel within the grass. Something about my size had made the passage, but a bird in the hand, so to speak, was more dangerous than a bird in the bush. Or whatever had scurried through this bush before me.

I continued to crawl until I couldn't see the bird before stopping. I tried not to pant but stress and running had done me in. Sitting, I stretched out my legs. I'd lost my stick, but I wouldn't complain about that now. If Throm hadn't grabbed me and taken us to the ground, I probably would no longer possess my head.

A shadow flew over me, low enough I could hear the flap of the wings, but I was nicely nestled within the rippling grass, and I doubted it could see me. Thankfully, the chef's outfits for the show were about the same color as the grass.

Eventually, the bird took off, cawing in irritation at its lost meal. I waited to the count of a hundred, then another hundred more, before crawling back through the passage to where I'd last seen Throm.

I rose to my shaky feet and, after making sure the bird wasn't lurking overhead, I peered around.

"Throm?" I whispered. Like he'd hear that? But I didn't want to call the bird's attention, let alone whatever made the passage through the grass. I swallowed, finding it hard to shove the spit down my dry throat. "Throm?" I squeaked in a slightly louder voice.

I was worried about him. What if he was hurt, lying in the grass bleeding. I'd never—

"Here." I whirled around to find him standing not far away, long pieces of grass caught in his hair. His color was high, but he wore a sexy smile on his face.

"Miss me?" he asked.

Half-sobbing, I raced toward him, leaping into his open arms, and wrapping myself around him.

He kissed me hard and fast, and if I wasn't worried

about hunting creatures, I'd drag him down into the grass and have my way with him. I needed our connection to show him how much he meant to me.

He lowered me to the ground and patted my ass. "All intact, I hope."

"You're okay?" I pawed his arms and belly until he started to laugh.

He grabbed my hands and kissed them. "I am fine."

"I don't know how we got away, but I'm grateful we did."

He peered toward the metal gleaming in the distance. "Dekrin said Jell wanted us to meet him on the other side of the forest, but I want to check that out instead."

"Jell wanted us to die in the forest."

"He's not one to let a slight go."

"I'm sorry," I said. "I should've left it alone."

He shrugged. "It's not your fault. He's a complete ass, and he deserved what he got and more."

"If I'd held onto my patience until the end of the show, then I could've head butted him."

"It was a joy to watch," he said with another grin. He tilted his head toward the gleaming metal. "Care to take a walk across the plain with me, love?"

Love, huh? I searched his gaze, finding only warmth there. "I thought you'd never ask," I croaked, overcome with emotions I couldn't quite define.

He leaned in close as we strode through the grass. "I don't always ask." He flashed me a smile that melted my bones. "More often, I just take."

38

THROM

We reached the edge of the plain and started up a long slope. I'd spied a flat surface at the top and suspected this was where we'd find Jell and the crew.

"Don't let on about the forest or the bird," I said softly.

"I like the idea of playing with Jell," she said with a sly smile.

And I liked the idea of conspiring with Wren. But as soon as we reached the top, and assuming my suspicion was correct, the next event would begin.

Only one of us would come out the winner.

"If this is it," she said softly when we were halfway up the slope, "I'm going to do my best, and I want you to do the same."

"I won't throw the game," I said.

"And I won't either. Whichever of us wins will do so because we hit the dish just right."

"If you win, I want you to send me a vid of the meals you prepare for the prince and his lovely bride, plus vids of the creatures at the shelter."

"And I want you to send me vids of your meals, plus you with your sister."

"I'll hand deliver them," I said, feeling as if the world was spinning out of control, dragging my heart along with it. One of us winning while the other lost wouldn't mess up what we'd started, would it? "I'm coming for you after when this is over, Wren. Never doubt that."

Voices echoed from the top of the hill. We were right to head in this direction.

"I think I'd track you down myself if you don't," she said. The soft smile on her face held a wealth of promise. "I'd kiss you for good luck, but I bet camera bots are watching already."

"I'd do the same."

I held out my fist, and she tapped it with hers. A friendly gesture that in no way could be considered fraternization.

We climbed the rest of the hill and walked out onto a big open, smooth-stone area.

Jell's back was to us, and he floated on his hover jet, giving direction to a drone.

Our shoes crunched on loose gravel.

"There you are," Jell said, turning to face us. "I was beginning to believe you were forfeiting the last match of the show."

"Sorry we took so long," Wren said with a bright smile. "We stopped to pick flowers on the plain, and then we got distracted by some gorgeous blue creatures lumbering through the forest."

I noted the net stretching over the cooking areas that would keep the birds from attacking. He'd known, and he'd been willing to let us die down there or in the forest.

The glare I sent him should've sliced him in two.

He huffed but pressed on a smile for the future viewers. "Now that you've arrived, it's time for the last episode of . . . Interstellar Chef!"

"I need a drink of water," Wren said.

Jell shook his head in mock dismay. "There won't be time for that. You're late, and the show is about to commence. You are welcome, of course, to quit, and I'm sure someone in the crew could provide you with water."

"There is no show without us. Water, please," I said.

"And that's where you're wrong." Jell chuckled and grinned at the closest camera bot. "You know on Interstellar Chef that we savor throwing out a twist here and there, right viewers?"

He'd done that by dropping us off in the wrong location.

"I do like to keep the chefs guessing," Jell added. "But I won't draw out the suspense for our delightful audience."

Fake applause and cheers erupted.

"Without further ado, allow me to show you the twist." He soared upward as a small transport pod landed between us and the cooking stations on the opposite end of the large stone plain.

The pod landed and the engine shut down.

When the hatch opened, Omyn hopped out.

"Welcome back, oh defeated one," Jell crowed.

Omyn's multi-toothed grin faltered, but he shored it up when he caught us gaping.

He sauntered over to us. "I called back," he said. "Whoever win today take all." He leaned in close. "By way, I send hidden camera bot wit you last night. Hope you not lying about fraternization."

39
WREN

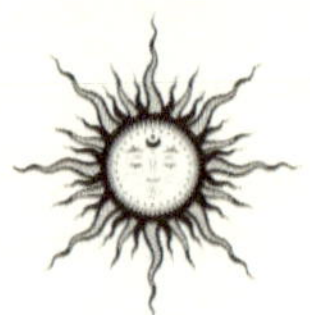

It was time to head butt Omyn, but I'd already made Jell hate me. No need to add Omyn to the mix.

Not that he needed a reason. Anger seemed to be his favorite emotion.

"Let's do this," Throm said, fury charging through his voice. I imagined he was as eager to shove Omyn off a cliff, but he held himself back. "There will be water at the cooking station."

I gave him a sharp nod.

"Welcome back, everyone," Jell shouted for the audience. "As you can see, Omyn is today's twist. He's back with full privileges. If he wins, he'll collect the money and the opportunity to prepare the luxurious, glorious, stupendous meal to culminate Crown Prince Lordenfeer's wedding." He swept in front of us on his hover jet, remaining far enough back I couldn't kick him.

Really, I wouldn't do something like that.

Okay, it was something I wanted to do more than anything, but I'd restrain myself.

"Please, please," Jell said, all jolly. "Don't be shy, Thrombuka and Wren. Join Omyn while I finish sharing my excitement with our lovely viewers."

We moved over to stand with Omyn, though we kept some distance between us. If I knew him, he'd attack rather than try to outcook us. And with Jell still pissed off about my actions, he'd do nothing to stop Omyn from killing us.

"For today's event, you'll prepare breakfast for our amazing judges waiting on a ship orbiting the planet," Jell said. "It's early in the morning, so breakfast feels right for the last event, doesn't it?" His sly glance darted to Omyn. Had they done something to ensure he'd win? "You'll each have two horas to complete your offerings."

Two hours? What kind of breakfast did he think we'd prepare that needed to take that long? My mouth went dry, and goosebumps broke out on my arms despite the heat, but I wasn't sure why I was suddenly nervous.

Jell nodded pertly. "I believe it's time to get started. I can't wait to share our mystery ingredient."

I studied the cooking stations, trying to find the trick. A net overhead would keep the birds from attacking. The stations were equidistant from each other and not so close that Omyn could "accidentally" eviscerate me while going to the chillers for ingredients. Bins waited beneath each station, and the chillers had been set up in front of the stone cliff at the end of the plain.

While Jell mentioned our numerous sponsors, I leaned close to Throm. "What's the catch?"

He shook his head. "I'm not seeing it yet but be careful. Only one contestant has died during this season, which isn't the norm."

Sometimes, none of the chefs made it home alive.

Why had I agreed to do this? Oh, yeah, prestige and money.

Back on the space station and while facing my fuming boss, the opportunity had sounded amazing. I'd shrugged off the idea that I could die during the show. Surely, they didn't actually kill chefs. They pretended to do so and gave each loser a small prize to make up for frightening the contestant's families.

"Are you ready, chefs?" Jell cried out. "On one, I want you to claim a cooking station. Three . . . Two . . ."

A cluster of shadows passed over us. I cringed, watching as a large flock of enormous birds circled overhead.

"One," Jell bellowed.

Throm and Omyn darted for the platform on the other side of the stone plain, and I came to my senses and took off after them.

Throm claimed the center—no surprise there—and Omyn grabbed the right side. I hopped up onto the platform and stood in front of the grill on the left, peeking around, while hoping to find a clue about the mystery ingredient. Breakfast, huh? I could aim for sweet or savory or a mix of both.

Both might be best, to give the judges a solid array of choices.

My mind returned to the conversation with Throm. If there was yeast in the chillers, I could prepare something with almost any mystery ingredient. Pancakes, an omelet. Hmm. So many good ideas.

Jell soared across the area in front of us. "Are you ready for your mystery ingredient, chefs?"

The fake audience roared in excitement.

Jell backed away from us. "The mystery ingredient is . . ." He pointed to the birds circling overhead. "Minzer eggs!"

Minzer eggs . . .?

An egg would work, but . . . I pawed through the boxes and ran to the chillers.

"No eggs," I cried. "Where are the eggs?"

"If you cannot find them, it appears you will need to collect them," Jell said with a smirk.

I gulped, looking up at the birds who'd be happy to grab and eat us.

Omyn leaped up and grabbed hold of the net. He shifted along the mesh to the edge and scrambled up onto the top.

As the birds cawed and dove toward him, he lifted his arms.

A bird swooped low and grabbed him in its claws. It soared back up into the sky and flew across the top of the long range of mountains.

I gaped at Throm.

"They have nests in the cliffs, I bet." His grim gaze met mine. "We could follow the birds to their nests, or . . ."

"No," I said, backing until my butt hit my cooking station. "It's impossible." A word I'd ditched from my vocabulary when I was sixteen and facing a future without my mom.

"This is why we have so much time to cook. We can do it." Throm rushed toward me and grabbed my arm. After hustling me over to the edge of the cooking platform, he lifted me up until I could grab onto the edge of the net.

"What keeps them from dropping us, then following to rip apart our twitching, dying carcass?"

"Don't let them do that."

"Sure, I'll tell them not to." I'd made it to the final event, and panic was charging through my soul.

"Hold onto the bird's ankles," he said.

"I don't know, Throm," I squeaked, my legs dangling as I clung to the net.

"You've got to, Wren. The quickest way to get an egg is to let one of them take you back to its nest."

40
THROM

I didn't want to let Wren handle this alone. Was there any way I could help her?

Fuck this show.

Fuck the no fraternization rules.

And fuck Jell.

I jumped and grabbed onto the net, easily levering myself up onto the upper surface. I reached down and grabbed Wren's wrist to haul her up beside me.

"Hold onto me," I said.

"What?"

"Grab on quick." A glance overhead showed the rest of the birds diving toward us. Whoever got here first would latch onto me with its claws. "Wrap your arms around me and hold on. We're doing this together."

"We can't."

"Remember what Jell said? We can help each other. Jell can't change his mind mid-show."

"Excuse me," Jell said as Wren leapt onto me and clung. She slid her arms around my neck, locking her fingers, and wrapped her legs around my chest.

"I like you in this position," I said with a grin.

She laughed, though it came out shrill. "I bet you do."

"You're not allowed to do this," Jell said. "She must obtain her own egg."

"Where does it say that in the rules, Jell?" I asked, then lifted my voice for the viewers. "Nothing says Wren and I can't get our eggs together, right?"

Someone behind the scenes must have been on our side because they hit the switch and the audience roared its approval.

"See?" I asked. The birds were almost upon us. "You might want to back away, Jell, or you'll be on your way to collect your own egg."

He growled but spun and flew to a safer location beneath the net.

"Ready?" I asked Wren.

"What if I say no?"

"Too late."

A bird latched onto my shoulders, and like I'd suggested Wren do, I grabbed onto its ankles. It took off, soaring into the sky. When it turned to the right, it flew along the top of the peaks, taking us away from the cooking platform. Like I'd guessed, it swooped lower and dove along the face of a cliff, slowing before landing on a wide ledge. A nest constructed of sticks and fur held three eggs.

My guts relaxed. I wasn't sure what I'd do if there was only one egg.

When the bird flow over the nest, I let go.

We dropped and landed hard in the nest, my foot crunching down hard on one of the eggs.

"Two left. Grab one," I said, my lungs on fire. I had to get Wren out of here before the bird landed and started shredding us for its meal. The eggs hadn't hatched, so it wouldn't leave us to rot for the hatchlings' first course.

Wren dove onto an egg, wrapping her arms around it. She rose to her knees and tucked her tunic into the top of her pants, stuffing the egg inside her shirt.

I did the same.

"We're outta here," she said, scrambling over the side of the nest and landing hard on her butt on the ledge below. As she jumped to her feet and backed against the side of the cliff, she peered up at me. "Get cookin' Throm, or you're about to be scrambled."

I laughed, loving how she'd turned a tense situation into something related to cooking.

No, I *loved* her. The feeling had crept up on me fast, but there was no denying the emotion making my heart flop in my chest. Did she feel the same?

"Do you love me, Wren?" I asked, clutching the side of the nest and looking down at her.

"Bad timing, Throm." She pointed behind me. "Incoming."

"Do you love me?"

"Throm. Please! Jump down here."

"Just answer?" I put my heart into my words. Surely she could hear it.

"I do, Throm, but if you don't get your ass down here pronto, I'm going to get pissed off."

I leapt over the side of the nest and landed easily in front of her. Grabbing her shoulders, I tugged her close and while I wanted to kiss her silly, I settled for a non-fraternization-style hug. "This is a promise of so much more."

"You've got it."

"We've got to get out of here, Wren," I said in all seriousness.

"Yup." Her grin sunk into my skin, heating me up fast.

I took her hand, and we raced to the edge of the ledge. Our arms spiraled as we looked down.

"I'm not jumping," Wren said. Turning, she squinted up. "But I think we can reach the top."

It wasn't far.

"How are you with climbing?" I asked as we raced back to the side of the cliff.

"I'm about to find out."

"Jump onto my back and hold on."

Her head tilted. "How are *you* with climbing?"

"I'm also about to find out."

"No reason for both of us to fall." She smacked my ass. "Get going, chef. I'm right behind you."

The bird screeched overhead, diving toward us with its claws extended. It would pluck us off the cliff, and this time, there would be no escape.

"Go first," I said, urging her in front of me. I could shelter her with my body. As a precaution, I grabbed a rock off the ledge, and when the bird was only a short distance away, threw the rock hard.

It smacked against the bird's head, and the creature spiraled to the right, smacking into the side of the nest.

"Go while it's distracted," I said. I hefted her up and held her until she'd grabbed onto a root sticking out of the side of the wall. She tucked the tip of her shoe into a decent-sized hole to help hold herself in place. I released her, and she started climbing.

I followed, not sparing a glance at the bird. It would come after us or it wouldn't. Watching wouldn't prevent it from happening.

I remained beside Wren as we climbed, and I was grateful the cliff sloped so it wasn't a vertical climb.

"No hugging the wall," she puffed out as she grabbed onto a root and scrambled to find footing. "Don't want to crush your egg."

"Better a crushed egg than a crushed us."

"You know what I mean."

We were halfway up the cliff.

Caws from overhead drew my eye. Other birds flew in circles, but they didn't swoop down, either respecting the territory of the bird who'd grabbed us or because they were afraid I could have another rock.

A glance down showed the bird I'd hit still sitting on the ledge. It watched us with anger shining in its eyes. Once it recovered, it would come after us, and I had a feeling it wouldn't stop until it had found revenge.

Chills grabbed hold of my spine and shook it. "Go faster," I hissed.

"Tryin'."

We kept climbing, soon reaching the top. Rather than stop to catch our breath, we ran, taking a trail that cut through the thick grass. We raced down the side of a slope and continued up the other side, remaining at the top of the peaks.

"I see the cooking stations," Wren crowed, pointing.

With her hair askew and her cheeks bright red, plus sweat making her face glow, she was the prettiest person I'd ever seen.

And she loved me. The feeling settled in my heart like a warm blanket. I wanted to hug it close. No, hug her. I would as soon as I could.

"You're my mate," I said.

"Last I heard . . . you haven't . . . proposed."

"I was getting there."

She flashed me a smile and kept running. "Hold that thought until this is over?"

"I'm not backing down." I held out my wrist, showing her the symbol, but I could tell by the scrunch of her brow she didn't understand. That was okay; I'd explain soon.

I spied the cooking area ahead.

Not long now and we'd be relatively safe beneath the net. How much time had passed? Could we still craft a dish?

Movement on the cooking platform drew my eye. Omyn was already hard at work with a pan on the heat conductor and ingredients out on his chopping block.

"Faster," Wren cried, roaring down the final slope. A glance at the timer showed we still had a little more than a horus. So, half our time left.

We'd almost reached the net when a shriek rang out above.

A bird flew straight for us.

It grabbed the back of Wren's shirt and flapped its wings hard, lifting her off the ground.

41
WREN

Throm latched onto my ankles and yanked.

The bird let go, and I plunged down, smacking into Throm. We tumbled to the ground, curling around our eggs.

I jumped to my feet. With Throm beside me, we raced beneath the net, not stopping to check if our eggs were broken.

A caw rang out as the bird swooped low and landed above us on the net.

I gave the bird the middle finger and ran to the cooking platform. No time for social niceties, birdie.

We raced around to the back of our stations. I reached into my tunic, hoping I wouldn't encounter goo, though I hadn't felt wetness against my skin.

When I pulled out a pristine, uncracked egg, I danced in a circle, holding it close to my chest. "It's safe. It's safe!"

Throm lifted his, showing his had made it through the fall, as well.

We got to work.

What to make? You'd think I could've decided that

while climbing the cliff. I'd also been dizzy due to my proximity to Throm. He loved me! He'd called me his mate. I couldn't wait to see what would come for us next.

But it was time to win this contest. I loved him, but that didn't mean I'd hand him the prize.

I flashed him a grin that must reveal my competitive spirit, and he answered it with one of his own.

A souvlette might be nice. I ran to the chillers, hip checking Omyn to the side when he tried to keep me from opening a door.

"Beat it," I added. "I'm on a roll."

"You late. I been back twenty minues."

"I still have an hour. Plenty of time to make a breakfast that'll knock yours out of the game."

He snarled, but he'd never been good with comebacks.

I grabbed a small carton of boulon cream and two sticks of stiller. I'd grate a bit of the latter's tough rind into my mix.

What else? A souvlette alone should impress the judges solely because they were a challenge to get just right, but I wanted to finish my plate with a few other items. I squinted into the chillers, but nothing sparked my interest.

I'd started back to my station to check out the totes beneath, but I tripped, landing hard on my knees.

Omyn cackled and tucked one of his long arms behind his back. "Clumsy, aren't you, human?"

Throm's growl ripped through the area, and all the color left Omyn's face. He scurried back to his station where something was smoking, and not in a good way.

"Burn your egg?" I asked tartly as I rose to my feet and raced to my station. I placed the cream and stiller on my chopping surface and ducked down, pawing through the boxes beneath.

Ah, yes, this herb would add sweetness. And brysson, sliced thinly and fried, would be lovely on the side. I'd sauté some oolons and fylers. I ran back to the chillers and grabbed fresh haffa berries to simmer with a little sweetener. I'd dribble the sauce on the plate, and it would taste as amazing with the salty brysson and the souvlette.

Camera bots zipped around us, taking in our expressions from every angle. If one got close, I'd be tempted to swat it. Although, I did want to impress my viewers. Surely someone was betting on me.

The next time a bot flew near, watching as I carefully removed the pits from the berries, I grinned at the camera. "I am going to blow the judges out of the water," I said with a grin.

"Not supposed injure judges," Omyn said, busily working at his station. He'd rescued whatever he'd burned and had begun plating.

"It means impress them," I said, though I didn't need to explain anything to him.

He grunted and kept working.

A glance at the clock told me I had less than forty minues left. I carefully lifted the egg and cracked it over a bowl, my eyes widening as the bright pink insides landed with a plop.

In no time, I'd whisked it up with the other ingredients and poured it into a greased pan. I popped it into the synth-oven and checked the time. It would be done in fifteen minues. With twenty left after that, I could allow it to cool without falling before plating it.

I got to work on the berries and brysson. Heady smells soon filled the air.

Throm had started plating, but I couldn't tell what he was making.

Omyn stirred something in a pan on his heat conductor, sashaying his butt while humming an off-key tune.

I ran to the chiller for zimmer juice. The tartness would make a nice contrast to the berries, though I'd only use a few drops.

When I returned to my station, the berries I'd left simmering on the heat conductor were gone.

42
THROM

Omyn raced toward me with a saucepan in his hand and a grin that bared his three rows of jagged teeth.

As he passed me, I plucked the saucepan from his hands.

"I'll take that, thank you very much," I said.

"Mine. Mine!" he said, hopping and trying to reach the pan I held over my head.

"It is not," Wren said, skidding to a stop in front of me. "He stole my berries."

"No steal," Omyn shouted. "No steal."

"Here you go." I started to give her the pan.

"Cheat. Cheat!" Omyn leaped onto Wren, and they tumbled to the ground.

There was no way she could fight off a six-armed Sevest warrior. I dropped the pan onto my chopping board and ran toward them.

Wren bucked and kicked out.

Omyn went flying, landing hard on his ass and skidding across the stone. He gaped at her. "What you do?"

With fury in her eyes, Wren jumped to her feet. "I grew

up on a space station. I lived in a crappy neighborhood. It's going to take more than you to knock me down." She gave him a cocky nod and sauntered to my chopping block, where she scooped up her pan of berries. "Thanks, Throm. Appreciate it."

Omyn and I watched her sashay back to her station with equally incredulous expressions.

I knew she was strong, but I'd thought most of her strength was centered in her will. She was kickass too. Why hadn't I seen it?

Knowing she didn't need me to hover over her and protect her only made me love her more.

"Twenty minues," Jell called out. "You should be close to plating!"

"My souvlette," Wren crowed, carefully lowering the dish onto the cooler. She leaned in close to the pan. "You are one awesome looking baby." Whirling, she started placing strips of something on her plates.

I did the same, carefully lowering one of my special donuts on each plate, then topping them with a sprinkle of kechar dust that made them sparkle. The dust would pop in their mouths when they bit into the donut, and a sweet kick would follow.

I added the rest of my offerings as the clock ticked down.

Omyn groaned and glared at his plates.

Something on one of them had caught fire. Had he experimented with one of the fiery ingredients from this planet? That would teach him to pay attention to his own dishes and stop trying to mess with ours.

Jell started counting down from ten, and when he reached one, he lifted his arms. "Stop! Your time is finished, chefs. If your dishes are not ready, then this is how it must be." He soared over us on his hover jet and examined each of our offerings. "Amazing. Simply amazing!"

Wren shot me a grin, her gaze taking in my dishes. "Looks great," she mouthed.

Win or lose, I was proud of what I'd made. I couldn't have cooked anything better.

"I'm so excited to see what happens next, aren't you?" Jell cried.

The fake audience screamed.

With a grin, Jell drifted to the center of the platform and came to a stop. "It's time to send your dishes to our judges."

Hover beams shot down from the sky, engulfing each of my plates. They disappeared in a flash, sucked up to the orbiting ship, and I leaned back on my heels, crossing my arms on my chest.

The final event was over.

Would I win this round, or would the catering job and money be awarded to Wren or Omyn?

43
WREN

While we waited to find out who had won the final round, Jell soared around—though he remained safely beneath the net.

I fisted my hands at my sides, my body a mess of nerves now that the end was here. I'd done the best I could.

I didn't know how I felt about all this. If I won, I'd be able to start a new life with the prize money and still have enough to set the shelter up financially until I found a new job. Then I could send credits when I had them, rather than think of them scrounging to buy food for the creatures.

And the catering job. It would give me the boost I'd sought since I took my first cooking job at a small diner in the dingiest part of the space station.

My new life would be so much better than the one I'd grown up in. I'd finally feel worthy of calling myself chef.

I would be somebody, when all my life I've been no one. I'd move to a new place where I'd have a name nobody knew. This would give me the ability to hold my head high. It was something I'd wanted since I was about three and my mom was caught for shoplifting. I'd sat in the store's control center, quaking.

Getting away from that was a future I'd clung to. I'd thought it was unattainable. Back on the station, I was the drunken thief's daughter. A scabby-kneed kid who was the prime suspect whenever something was stolen. Who everyone thought would turn out no different than her mother.

But if I won, Throm would not be able to fulfill his dreams, and I hated the thought of that. He'd done amazing things with his restaurant. The catering job would give him the chance to level up in a way he never could've imagined. He was as ambitious as me, and I was confident he'd get where he hoped to be all on his own, but the catering job would give it to him right away.

I knew what it was like to crave success, and I didn't want to take it from him.

As for the money, he needed it to help his sister. How worthy was that? The creatures needed me, but I wasn't their only benefactor. They had a trust and some of the wealthy ladies on the space station brought in bags of food and supplies. They *could* get by without me.

Would Throm's sister get by without prize money to set her up in the life she needed?

That was it. I *wanted*. She *needed*.

Maybe it was time I faced the fact I was doing okay already. I'd worked in some amazing jobs, and my dishes were renowned in my tiny corner of the multi-universe.

I'd been selected to compete on Interstellar Chef. How many cooks out there dreamed of getting into the show but never received the call?

Throm loved me. That gave me a warm, mushy feeling inside, like his arms were always around me. I didn't know where we were going, but I had a feeling we'd do so together.

So, here I stood on the platform with Throm shooting me encouraging looks. Even in this, he supported me, boosting me up. I'd told him about my past, and he still saw me as someone worth fighting for.

Caws rang out overhead, and I peered through the netting, watching as they circled. They'd attack, given the first chance.

"Ah, yes," Jell said. "Interesting. Interesting." His gaze scanned me and the other two waiting for the results, and I swore mischief lurked on his face.

What was he planning now? He'd do anything to make sure I didn't win, and I imagined he felt the same about Throm. And if Throm or I won, Jell would make sure we didn't live long enough to claim the prize.

I'd always thought the point of this show was to discover new talent, to give those of us who dream a chance.

Now it appeared the show was all about making sure as many of us lost as possible. My shoulders drooped as one emotion after another roared across my heart.

Throm looked ready to leap over to me and give me a big hug, but I needed to contain this feeling on my own.

It was natural to put a lot of hope in a show like this. If I focused on what I wanted, recognition, I could tell myself I was a success no matter what the outcome.

With that thought in mind, I straightened my spine and sent Throm a reassuring smile. He nodded and studied my face for a few secunda before turning his attention to Jell.

"If you would line up, please," Jell said. "We will announce the winner shortly. First, however, I'd like to share the judge's comments. Omyn, Omyn, Omyn." Jell soared over to the Sevest warrior and patted his back. "The judges had so many glowing things to say. One even literally glowed due to the special ingredient you included in your dish. So clever." His low chuckle rang out and the fake audience snickered.

What ingredient made a judge glow? I glanced at Throm, but he shrugged, turning his intent gaze back to Jell.

"Such a wonderful offering you prepared, Omyn," Jell said. "Your dishes received rave reviews from the judges. Your hard-boiled egg was just the right presentation in the scalloped half-shell. And your sides! One judge commented he had never tasted a cavast tart like yours. You light touch of seasoning with the kartoffs, combined with just enough heat from the puriander flakes topped off your dish. Well done."

I gulped, feeling like it was over already. When I contemplated losing, it was to Throm. It would be easy to smile and congratulate him, because him winning didn't mean I'd lost.

But Omyn? Ugh. I hated to think he'd been booted off the show and now the victory would be handed to him.

It wasn't fair, but that was the point.

They brought him back to taunt us and to give the viewers an unexpected twist. Maybe even to run away with the prize.

"And Thrombuka," Jell said, soaring on his hover jet over to float in front of Throm. "The judges had wonderful things to say about your dish as well. One stated they hadn't ever tasted a poached egg as exquisitely prepared as yours."

Throm nodded; his arms linked across his chest.

You'd think Jell would take this chance to mock us, but

he was a showman first. He'd play with us when he was off air, but in front of the camera bots, he was an actor always.

"What was the herb you used in the sauce you delicately drizzled on your side of zilar?" Jell asked. "A judge would like to know. He couldn't quite place it."

"I used an herb that grows in the mountains of this planet called foosier. It's rare, but I spied some while collecting my egg. I've used it before. The sauce is my own creation."

"Wonderful," Jell said. "The judge passes his compliments to you. He said he'd like to keep a bottle of the sauce in his chiller to use on a variety of dishes."

Throm tapped his forehead and dipped forward in a short bow. "Judge? I will make this sauce and ship it to you. Please get in touch with me after the show."

"As for you, Wren," Jell said with a scowl. He soared my way on his hover jet, stopping just before running into me.

Throm's growl ripped through the air.

Jell tipped his head back and laughed. "Just kidding. I'd never harm one of our chefs, right Wren?"

"Sure," I said sullenly, but I curved my lips up in a smile.

The audience cheered.

"I know you, Jell," I said. "You'd *never* do something like that."

His eyes went steely, but he was a good enough actor he could correct that within seconds. A cheery expression filled his face, and his eyes glowed with happiness. The camera bots zipped around us, recording our faces from all angles.

"As for your dish, one judge noted she'd never tasted a souvlette like yours before. It was perfectly crafted and baked. And another judge mentioned that you used just the right touch of spices. A bit sweet and a bit savory was a wise mix on your part. The boulon cream's light essence came through nicely. As for your side of brysson sauteed with fylers and oolons, one judge commented that he nearly fell off his pedestal when he tasted it. The haffa berries only added to the loveliness of your presentation, and they made the other flavors *pop*."

"Thank you, judges," I cried, waving, though I doubted they could see or hear me.

Whoa. Effuse praise. How was this contest going to turn out?

Jell flew backward until he could survey the three of us. "Well, I imagine you'd like to know who won, correct?"

The audience cheered.

"I'm not sure I can hear you," Jell said.

I rolled my eyes at Throm.

Really, get it over with, would you?

"It appears we have another tie," Jell said, his sly gaze passing from one of us to the next.

Omyn flexed his claws and crouched, ready to spring on whoever he'd tied with.

"The winners are Throm and Wren!"

44
THROM

Omyn's jaws dropped, and I wondered if he'd been told the fix was in. He glared at me and Wren, and it was clear from the hate churning across his face that he'd like to slash through us both. But he'd lost. It was not a three-way tie. Killing us wouldn't make him the winner.

He stalked toward us. "I have proof." He pointed right at us. "Fraternize. Fraternize!"

"What are you talking about?" Wren asked, backing toward me.

"Secret camera bot," he snarled. His hand swept toward a viewscreen mounted on the opposite side of the platform. "Watch."

The camera was some distance away, but anyone watching could clearly see me and Wren frolicking in the water at the pomgrole pools last night. Her back was to me, and she lay across the surface, her face filled with bliss. The water sloshed around us, but it did across most of the pool fed by the falls.

"See?" Omyn cried. "See what you do. Fraternization!"

"I'm lying on the water," Wren said, and it wasn't a lie. "It felt good."

Very good.

"My arms are nowhere near her," I said, also not a lie.

"You do . . . things," Omyn bellowed. "Many things. Watch."

The vid showed us walking to the falls.

"She's wearing clothing," I pointed out.

"See," Omyn said ominously. "You break rules. Kicked out show."

We walked beneath the falls.

I stood with Wren, and I loved how she lifted her chin and tried to stare Omyn down.

"I'm not seeing fraternization," Jell said. He actually scowled at Omyn. "You are wasting our time. You lost, and you must leave. That is the rule."

"Fraternization," Omyn cried again. "They break rules!" With a growl, he leaped and grabbed the edge of the net, tearing it from the ties holding it in place.

It fell as I dove toward Wren, rolling when we hit the stone platform. The net landed on top of us, tangling around us.

Jell bellowed, caught in the netting nearby. He toppled to the ground. His hover jets churned, trying to drive him through the net, and he cried out in pain.

A caw overhead was echoed by others. The birds dove toward us, their open beaks and claws extended.

"Watch out," Wren cried, struggling to rise to a crouch. The net draped over her, pinning her down, and she shoved at it futilely.

Jell looked up and shrieked.

Drones soared between him and the birds, shooting lasers toward the descending flock.

They cawed and swooped toward us instead, but with the net covering us, I doubted they could grab us.

Omyn was clear of the net, however, and the birds saw his vulnerability.

So did he, although he came to his senses too late. He whirled and bolted down the hillside, disappearing from view.

The birds followed, swarming over the edge of the cliff.

Omyn's brief scream rang out.

Then silence.

We shoved the net away.

I grabbed the end Omyn had removed from the metal awning and hooked it back in place. This tugged it off Jell.

He rose to his hover jet-clad feet and swayed before flying flew toward me and Wren.

"I thank you from the bottom of my heart for your efforts," he said, dipping his head toward me. "Should we return to the program?"

In the rush to remain safe, I'd forgotten that Wren and I had tied for the win.

"You must battle to determine who finishes first," Jell announced.

45
WREN

"I'm not fighting Throm," I said. "First of all, I wouldn't win, and second, I won't risk hurting him."

"And I won't fight her," Throm said.

"But there cannot be a tie," Jell cried. "You must battle."

I shrugged. "We won't." I turned to Throm. "Want to split the prize?"

A gleam appeared in his eyes. "What do you propose?"

"So many things, Throm," I said with a laugh that came out much too husky for a vid show. "*So* many things." All I could picture was being with him again, holding him and loving him for the rest of my days. He hadn't said he wanted forever with me, but I suspected he would. "As for the show, I've got an idea."

I crooked my finger, and he bent closer to listen to my explanation.

"I like it," he said, putting his arm around my waist and tugging me into his side.

"No fraternization allowed," Jell cried.

"The show is over. No rules apply to how we interact with each other after the end."

Jell's shoulders slumped. "You're right. I hadn't thought of that." We might've knocked him down for a secunda, but he rallied quickly, doing a quick backflip to draw the camera bots' attention. "I will remember this for the next show. How will you decide who wins?"

"We both do," I said. "I'll take a small share of the money and donate it to the creature shelter on the space station. Throm will use the rest to help his sister."

As for me needing money to buy respect, I'd earned that already. My worth came from who I was inside. I dared anyone to try to take that away.

"We're co-catering the prince's wedding," Throm said. "We'll also share that part of the prize."

"That is forbidden," Jell cried with glee, sure he'd won. "It has never been done before."

"It will be done now," Throm said with a growl.

Jell huffed. "You cannot make up your own rules. Only one of you will cater the event. Besides, the prince will never allow you both to prepare the meals for his and his intended's wedding reception."

"Oh, but I shall," someone said from behind him.

Dekrin, the pilot of the prince's ship, strode forward. "Don't you recognize me, Jell?" He yanked something over his head and tossed it aside.

I frowned at the rubbery face lying on the ground before looking up at Dekrin. I'd only seen a few vids of the prince before, but it was him.

Jell gasped, and his arms flailed outward. His hover jet hissed, and for a secunda, I thought it would dump him. "Crown Prince Lordenfeer? But . . ."

The tall alien with lavender skin shot us a grin. "I love flying, but I don't often get the chance." His gaze fell on us. "When your shuttle was damaged, and I heard you needed someone to take you from one event to the next, I volunteered. I've always loved watching Interstellar Chef, and this gave me a front row seat to the show." His scowl took in Jell. "I did not approve of this . . . fiend's plan for what nearly happened to you in the forest." He bowed deeply. "I apologize."

"You, um, didn't do it." I sent my glare Jell's way. "He did that all on his own."

"I . . ." Jell sputtered. He tried for a backflip, but the hover jet failed, and he flopped onto his belly on the stone. Rising, he rubbed his chest and winced.

"I was watching, too," a woman said, striding over to Dekrin. She leaned into his side, gazing up at him with adoration. "But I think it's time to go home and get ready for our wedding, don't you, sweetheart?"

"I do. I cannot wait until I can claim you as my bride." He lifted her off her feet and kissed her.

Throm and I grinned at each other, savoring their love. I wanted to kiss him, but we'd already pushed Jell as far as we should. No need to rub our "fraternization" in his face.

Eventually, Crown Prince Lordenfeer lowered his future mate to her feet.

She waved at me. "You're catering our wedding? Yay! I'm Elys Maxwell, and I'm following this big purple brute around wherever he goes."

"Brute, eh?" He swept her up and soundly kissed her again.

When he put her down, her pretty cheeks were pink, and she couldn't stop shooting him longing glances. It was clear they were crazy about each other.

"Anyway," she said with a smile. "I was hiding in my prince's cabin." She pouted his way. "He loves to fly, but his personal entourage rarely lets him run free. He wanted to get to know the chef who would cater our wedding and talked the pilot into letting him fly the craft instead. Of course, I had to come, though I had to remain in hiding because you would've guessed who he was if you saw me strolling around on the ship."

I nodded, enthralled by her tale. To think she'd been on board the ship the entire time.

"Let me tell you," she said. "The suite on the ship is gorgeous, but I'm glad I'm no longer cooped up in there. Except when you visited me, right love?" She gave him a quick kiss, then smiled at me. "Wren, I can't wait to show you the palace. The gardens are particularly gorgeous, if I do say so myself."

"They are because of all my hard work," the prince said with a twinkle in his gorgeous green eyes.

"You." She playfully smacked his arm. "I'm the one who got rid of that pesky vine."

From what I recalled, she'd been hired to work as a landscaper in the palace grounds, and that was where she'd met the prince. She'd thought he was a fellow gardener at first, and from what I heard, all hell broke loose when she found out who he truly was. Imagine kissing the gardener —or whatever they'd done—then finding out he was actually your boss.

I couldn't wait to hear the rest of the story—from Elys herself.

My life was a dream. Imagine me being shown around the palace by the future mate of the Crown Prince of Nomir. Talking and chatting with her. It was going to be amazing.

"I can't wait," I gushed, barely able to catch my breath.

Elys winked, and I could tell I'd made a friend already. "The palace is amazing."

"As for them both catering?" The Crown Prince shot Jell

a scowl. "How dare you suggest these two stellar chefs fight for the honor of preparing our reception meal? If they work together, the meal will only be that much better." He bowed. "I'd be honored if you'd both prepare the meals for our reception."

"Definitely," Elys chimed in. Her lips twisted when she looked Jell's way. "Speak up, dude, and fast."

Jell dipped forward, over and over. "I apologize, Your Highness. And your soon to be Highness . . . err, Princess Elys. Of course Thrombuka and Wren will share the prize."

"Not just the catering part of the prize," the prince said with a lifted eyebrow. "I believe I heard Wren suggest a way of splitting the monetary prize as well?"

"You did," Jell said, his entire body sagging.

He'd been humiliated on camera, and I couldn't even drum up a speck of pity.

Okay, a tiny bit. I didn't like to see anyone feeling down, especially when I was so happy.

I turned to Throm and found him staring down at me with so much love in his gaze it made my body simmer.

"I really can't wait to be alone with you," I said. "Without camera bots watching."

"Same." He took my hands. "I have one more suggestion, something you didn't think of when we came up with our plan for the prizes."

"What's that?"

"What would you think of moving to my home planet and helping me open up another restaurant?"

"Throm, are you proposing I work for you?" I asked, unable to hold a stern face. "That would make you my boss."

"Actually, I was proposing a mating, love," he said

softly. "Will you be my forever mate, the only one I'll love for the rest of our days?"

"Yes, yes, yes," I cried, leaping into his arms.

The camera bots zipped in to film our happy moment, but I didn't care one bit.

My lips were on Throm's and his arms held me tight.

There was no one I loved more than my alien mate.

46

EPILOGUE
WREN

O*ne Lunar Cycle Later*

"I think your ass is on fire," Throm said, pointing.

Shit. I whirled around, but finding no fire near my person, I sent him a mock scowl.

"Just making sure you're on your toes," he said, swooping in close to me. He swept his arm around my back and tugged me up to give me a quick kiss before smacking my ass. "I forgot to grab some pearlung. If you have time, can you chop some and toss it in with the fylers?"

"On it." I zipped away from him and ran to the chillers lining the back of the enormous palace kitchen.

Today was the day we'd waited for. Crown Prince Grivvel, whose nickname was Dekrin, would soon be married to Elys, my new friend and confidant. In fact, I'd just gotten up the nerve to ask her to be my maid of honor when Throm and I get married in a few lunar cycles.

Married. Who would've thought when I signed up to

compete in Interstellar Chef that I'd fall in love and move to my new mate's home planet?

I'd sent a solid number of credits to the creature shelter, and they were set for food and supplies for at least a year. And with job offers coming in all the time now that we were catering this wonderful event, our plans to expand Throm's restaurant business looked fantastic. I would head up the catering end of things while he oversaw the management of the new restaurants while stopping in to cook on occasion when he got the urge to experiment with a new recipe he'd crafted. We might even prepare some Interstellar Chef style menus together.

His sister had left the rehab facility and moved into her new home. With extra care and physical therapy, she was great. She'd recently started dating an Earthling—who also happened to be her new physical therapist.

Our life couldn't get better.

"Ten minues," one of our palace staff assistants called out from the entry to the kitchen. "The Crown Prince and his lovely bride will be here in ten minues."

After grabbing the pearlung and setting it on a block for chopping, I raced to the chillers and helped the staff pull out trays of appetizers. We'd opted to include the dishes we'd made during the show, though we'd agreed to skip some of the more deadly ingredients, including minzer eggs.

I'd be happy if I never saw a big bird again.

Surprisingly enough, drones had gone after Omyn. He was a jerk, but I guess I didn't wish him death despite the fact that he would've tried to harm us. He was sent back to his planet and from what I'd heard, was milking his "injuries" and status from the show with all the local females.

Crik'ee was also alive. They'd faked his death for the audience, a gruesome thing to do. But the show wasn't live, so he was able to watch his supposed death with his family. With his cheerful personality, I assumed he'd find a way to profit from his loss too.

The show had a reputation of sending contestants home in body bags, which evidently wasn't true, except on the rare occasion. It would've been nice if someone had filled me in on that before it got started.

"They're here," someone cried out from the room beyond the kitchen. "They're here!"

I grinned at Throm. "They're married. I'm so happy for them." I would've liked to attend the wedding but preparing meals for my new friends' reception was just as much fun. I'd pop out of the kitchen later with Throm when Elys and Dekrin shared their first dance. They'd matefasted in the Nomir way this morning and followed the Nomir ceremony up with the usual Earthling ceremony with a justice of the peace wedding and now, a glorious reception.

While the guests and happy couple enjoyed the appetizers, we put the finishing touches on the first course. The staff would serve while we ensured the rest of the meal was ready.

We bustled around the kitchen for hours, sending out one wonderful offering after another until nothing was left but the piece de resistance—the wedding cake.

It looked so cute with the cake topper highlighting an animated bride and her beastly lavender-skinned alien groom. When she caught my eye, she winked. He bowed and swept her up, spinning her in a circle before returning her to her original position.

After the cake was wheeled out to the reception area,

Throm rested his back against a wall and crooked his finger my way. "Come give me kisses, mate."

"I'm always happy to oblige," I said, untying and tossing away my apron. I sauntered over to him, taking my time, but leapt on him when I was a few steps away.

He caught me, which was no surprise. This guy would never let me fall.

As his lips captured mine, I moaned and wrapped my arms around him.

There was no place better than being in a kitchen with my very own Interstellar Chef.

Ahh! I just love a sweet, tasty ending, don't you?

If you'd like to catch up with Wren & Throm,
I've written a bonus epilogue, and
it's your FR*EE when you sign up for my newsletter.
Wren is hungry, and Throm has just the
right dish in mind...
SIGN ME UP!

Elys and Dekrin's story,
Cultivating the Alien, is next.

Dekrin loves to sneak out of

the palace and work in the gardens.
Imagine Elys's surprise when she
discovers her fellow gardener,
the grubby, low-slung-pants-wearing alien
who's been cultivating her person fields, is
actually the Crown Prince of the alien kingdom.

Turn the page to get a peek at Chapter 1...

ABOUT THE AUTHOR

Ava Ross is a two-time *USA Today* Bestselling author of numerous titles, all of them featuring sweet and steamy romance. She fell for men with unusual features when she first watched Star Wars, where alien creatures have gone mainstream. She lives in New England with her husband (who is sadly not an alien, though he is still cute in his own way), her kids, and a few assorted pets.

SERIES BY AVA

Mail-Order Brides of Crakair

Brides of Driegon

Fated Mates of the Ferlaern Warriors

Fated Mates of the Xilan Warriors

Holiday with a Cu'zod Warrior

Galaxy Games

Alien Warrior Abandoned/
Shattered Galaxies

Beastly Alien Boss

Screamer Woods Shared World:
Orc Me Baby One More Time

Stranded With an Alien: Frost

You can find my books on Amazon.

CULTIVATING THE ALIEN

**My new job gives me the chance to put
my past behind me. Only one problem:
I'm falling for my boss...**

After my ex dumps my possessions on the sidewalk, cleans out our bank account, and steals my landscaping business, I'm once again submitting job applications. It's that or no roof over my head. With the Intergalactic Employment Agency's help, I land a position as a gardener for the owners of an off-world alien castle.

Other than needing to tackle a rogue vine infesting the front shrubs, it's an easy job. Best of all, I work alongside Dekrin, a dirty-mouthed fellow gardener who enjoys rolling in mud and wearing low-slung pants. His gardening skills are impressive, but I'm even more impressed by his attempts to plow my person field.

I'm falling for him, so who cares if I ever return to Earth? But after what happened with my ex, trusting my heart to

Dekrin won't be easy. Do I dare take a chance with a bad boy alien who I suspect is cultivating a big secret?

Cultivating the Alien is Book 4 in the Beastly Alien Boss Series. Each features an Earth woman hired for an off-world job who meets a gruff alien who can't resist falling for his fated mate.

Get Your Copy Now

CHAPTER 1
ELYS

"Welcome to the Intergalactic Employment Agency," the tall thin Udril male said, two smiles lifting his cheekbones. They gleamed in the overhead flurolights.

I stood just inside the door of the building, unable to believe I actually had to come here. "I'm looking for a job."

"Yes, yes, we're quite used to hearing that." His two smiles widened as he rounded the glass counter and strode toward me on cloven hooves. "Hence the name, *Employment Agency*." His chuckle faded when mine didn't join in.

Because I didn't want to be mean, I flashed him a smile, though it stretched my lips beyond where they'd been for months. "I *had* a job. A good one."

"I'm sure you did." One of his four arms gestured for me to come farther inside. "If you'll tell me your name, I'll look up your experience on the dash." The dash, a hovering computer screen, floated close behind him. Whirring, it evaded his spiked tail, whipping back and forth like the pendulum in the antique clock I used to own.

This was before my life abruptly fell apart, forcing me to sell all my worldly possessions to afford the deposit on an apartment the size of my former walk-in closet.

There was nothing like hitting rock bottom to make a woman rethink her past and her future.

"I'm Elys Maxwell," I said, adding my interstellar ID number we were all given at birth. "As you'll see when you pull up my history, I'm a certified landscaper. I've won awards. I own..." Pinching my eyes shut, I held back the bitter tears stinging my eyes. I'd cried too much about this already, and I refused to do it any longer. "I *used to* own my own landscaping business."

The funniest thing about my breakup with my ex was that I missed the business we'd built together more than him. He'd become a . . . challenge to get along with over the past year. I discovered why when I came home early one afternoon to find all of my possessions sitting on the stellarwalk in front of our house—and our joint bank balance cleaned out.

He'd used me and tossed me aside, saying he was bored with us, that he'd done all the work, and thus, he deserved to own it all. This is what I got for letting a guy set up our joint business and sign the paperwork for our new home. He'd put his name on everything, conveniently leaving mine off, and I'd been too gullible to look into it until it was too late.

Our business legally belonged to him, as did the house, and I had no credits to hire killer legal support. A friend working pro bono got me a too small lump settlement, and I'd had to sign off on the rest. I was told I was lucky to have received even that.

There was nothing I could do except move on, as gut-churning as the prospect might be.

At least he couldn't steal the skills I'd developed with plants and landscaping design. Good luck to him keeping the business successful, because every job he worked on was going to look clunky and boring. I was the one who'd turned our landscaping work into an art form.

"Okay, now," the Udril said, tapping a claw on the dash screen. "It says here you have gardening experience?"

"Landscaping." I moved closer to him. "There's a big difference."

"Oh, I'm sure there is."

"The two are actually similar," I gushed, warming up to the subject as always. "Gardening is more about cultivating the ground, while landscaping deals with the bigger picture, including planting trees and shrubs, redoing existing designs, and adding decorative components that make a garden shine."

"Ah, yes," the Udril said, his long lines of light blue brow ridges wiggling. "I'll be sure to include that difference in your job search, though it may narrow your options."

"I'll take what I can." It was that, or I didn't eat. I'd put off job-hunting for as long as I could.

"Would you prefer something off world or here on Earth?" he asked, his claws poised above the screen.

"Off-world if possible." Each day I remained here was another day where the work I'd done—and the pride I took in it—slapped me in the face all over again.

He tapped on the screen before looking up. "I have three jobs to offer you, Elys Maxwell."

"Just Elys."

His head dipped forward. "Elys, it is. The first is a landscaping position with an Aenid tribe. They're seeking someone to subdue a stressnoot overgrowth."

"I haven't worked with stressnoots before." I tilted my

head, and my long, black hair swished across my shoulders. I wore it up when I worked, but I liked to keep it down when things were casual. "Are stressnoots much of a challenge?"

"They rarely eat those sent to prune them."

My already-wan smile drooped. "What's the second job?"

"A Mowair warrior has constructed an ice palace on the planet Rivail. He needs someone to work in the gardens."

"Ice palace?" I asked. "It's literally built out of ice?"

"Yes, the entire planet is frozen, you see, and he used large chunks to craft the structure himself. Did you see the presentation on vid? They broadcasted it everywhere. Such a fete. It's very tall, and he placed the building on the largest glacier. Frankly, I'd love to—"

"What kind of landscaping would I do on an ice planet?" Sculpture wasn't my thing.

"That would be up to you, I suppose," the Uldin said, tapping his lower lip with a claw. "The position comes with a generous salary, though there are a few tiny conditions."

"Such as?"

"The imported plants must not die, or you will be punished. And you will be required to warm the Mowair's furs."

"Like, warm them up for him?" I wasn't exactly sure what the latter entailed.

"Not exactly," the Uldin coughed, "You would be expected to grant him sexual favors."

My lips twisted. "Is this the norm with off-world positions?"

"It's not that unusual. As I said, this position comes with a few conditions. It's been quite a challenge to find someone for this job, but the salary is exceedingly generous.”

“I don’t want to sleep with anyone.”

He glanced down his long, pointed nose at me. “I doubt there would be much sleeping in this job. Mowairs are considered quite . . . vigorous.”

No way would I take a job that required me to sleep with the boss. It was bad enough I’d slept with my co-owner. Maybe if I hadn’t, I would’ve paid more attention to the business aspect of our relationship.

“What’s the third job?” I asked.

“I’m afraid it’s not nearly as glamorous as the Mowair position.”

I tapped my foot. “Let me decide about that.”

“The Lordenfeer family on the planet Nomir are seeking a base-level gardener.”

So, not a landscaping position, but maybe I could work my way up. I wasn’t opposed to hard work. In that, I shined. “Who are the Lordenfeers?”

“The royal family of the small planet. They rule over a vast community.”

“Are they jerks?” I asked.

“I don’t believe so.”

“What’s the pay?”

He named something decent enough for an entry-level gardening position. “It also includes room and board. You’ll have your own small cottage and will take meals with the other staff.”

I could sublet my apartment and save credits—a big bonus right there.

“I won’t be required to warm the king’s bed furs, I hope,” I said.

"No, you will not be asked to have sex with anyone. I should add that this job is long term. They require a one-yaro commitment. It seems they keep losing gardeners."

"Why?"

He shrugged, all four arms lifting. "They've had a few issues with a rogue vine that keeps consuming the flowers and attacking anyone who tries to enter the front of the castle."

"I can handle rogue vines," I said, warming to this job. It would get me off Earth and it was long term. I'd have plenty of time to forget about my ex. The burning in my belly would finally ease. "I'll take the third job."

"Lovely," the Uldin said, scooting back behind the counter. "Would you like to leave now or tomorrow?"

"So soon?"

"This position has been open for a very long time."

With rogue vine issues, I could understand.

Some might consider this running away. A few of my friends wanted me to fight my ex, to make him give me my fair share of the business. But sometimes, a woman had to admit defeat and move forward.

It was time for me to start over.

"I can leave tomorrow," I said. One of my friends would handle my apartment while I was gone.

"Very well. I'll send a shuttle to your residence at six in the morning sharp."

A real smile lifted my lips for the first time since my ex kicked me out two months ago. "Perfect."

That night, I stuffed a bag with clothes and a few personal items. When the shuttle arrived bright and early the next morning, I dropped my bag inside the upper compartment of the vessel and climbed into the main chamber. The hatched closed, and the sickly sweet gas I vaguely remembered from the last time I'd taken a stasis flight swept across my face.

I'd only traveled in stasis a few times, and each time I woke up, I acted drunk. Fortunately, the effect wore off quickly.

When the ship touched down on Nomir, it woke me. Just the other times, my head spun, and I had an inane urge to laugh. This time, however, my body tingled, like the time I'd bathed in a loosh pool while on vacation. How was I supposed to know loosh water was slick with an aphrodisiac? I'd traveled alone, and it hadn't been easy riding out the loosh pool effect by myself.

I stretched inside the shuttle as it powered down, luxuriating in the warm, aroused feeling coursing through me. My ditzy brain told me it didn't mind this additional side effect of stasis one bit.

The hatch opened, and I sat up, peering around. The craft had touched down on the edge of the Lordenfeer kingdom. A castle constructed of shiny, pale gray stone surrounded by elaborate gardens loomed not far away.

An alien with four arms stood on scaffolding, using what looked like wire brushes to clean the stone.

"Ah, you've arrived," someone said, calling my attention away from the building. "Welcome. You must be Elys. I'm Dekrin."

I turned in his direction, and my jaw dropped.

A dark purple god stood nearby, dressed in nothing but low-slung pants he'd rolled up to reveal his dark purple, hairy calves. His feet were bare and coated in pale green dirt, and he held a clump of limp dessier grass in his hand. Green dirt smeared his lightly haired, muscular torso and painted his chiseled face. Even his long black hair threaded through with silver bands and pulled back at his nape hadn't missed out on the mud fest. Had he been rolling in it?

Truly, I wouldn't mind mud wrestling with this guy. Wait, no, the grass he held suggested he was a fellow *gardener*.

I snickered. He could plow my personal fields any day of the week. I barely stifled my giggle at the thought. My throbbing body told me exactly what garden I wanted him to cultivate.

He was a hired hand like me, however. We'd soon be friends. Best buds, maybe.

Even in my stasis-induced lusty phase, I didn't want to do or say anything that would embarrass me later.

However, I had a feeling he could make me forget all about my ex.

"Yes, I, uh . . . I've arrived," I said, struggling to sound normal. I scrambled over the side of the shuttle and clung to the side to keep from plopping on the ground.

"Steady there." He strode closer, concern creasing his pretty face. Reaching out, he grabbed onto my arm. "You don't want a mishap."

Perhaps I did.

The warmth of his fingers sparked across my skin, and I didn't even mind the subtle bite of his claws.

Hooyah my belly shouted. Other girly parts of me joined in, thrumming with excitement.

Etchings rippled across the tall alien's chest and arms as if he had a living tattoo. They drew my eye, and I couldn't drag my gaze from the glorious display.

Frowning, I reached out to touch them.

"You don't look good," he said, grabbing my hand to hold me steady. "I think I should get you to your cabin. You can lay down, sleep it off."

"You're right. I need a bed."

Still holding onto me, he reached into the shuttle, grabbing my bag and hefting it onto his shoulder. "I'll show you where to go. After you've rested, we can discuss what will be expected from you on the job."

"Are you my . . ." I hiccupped. "My new boss?"

"More or less."

"Then we'll be . . . tackling each other?" My brain sure didn't want to function like it should. When I burped, I slapped my hand over my mouth. "Excuse me. I mean tackling rogue vines together. Not tackling each other."

Watching me, his lips quirked up on one side. "You're not a fan of tackling things other than vines?"

"It depends on what kind of vine I'm tackling." Damn, but my brain kept rolling with the innuendo. I really needed to sleep this off. As tempting as my new boss, or coworker, or whatever he was, might be, I wasn't interested in getting involved with anyone new. The wounds delivered by my ex had only recently scarred over.

His gorgeous eyes sparkled. "Let's see how you feel when you're no longer under the influence of stasis, all right? Then we can talk about vines and other kinds of tackling."

As he hustled me away from the shuttle, it took off, soaring into the sky. We wove through the gardens, and it was all I could do to place one foot in front of the other.

Each step created friction between my legs and made my brain buzz.

"You smell good," I lisped.

He flashed me a smile full of very sharp teeth. "Thanks. You smell good yourself."

I swore he was laughing, but this was a serious discussion.

"Do you always bathe in mud?" I asked.

His chuckle rang out. "Sometimes." His voice deepened. "Does it bother you to get muddy?"

"Not in the least."

"Good, because this job is hands on."

"I should hope so."

I needed to stop thinking of how hands-on I'd like him to be.

He led me along the back of the castle, and I gaped at the enormity of it, taking up a few city blocks. It towered over me with one, two, three, no, four stories. A railed walkway wove across the top. I'd love to check it out. The view of the mountains must be amazing from up there.

"What I meant was, this job will get you dirty," he said. "But we have plenty of water here, unlike drier planets. There are real showers in each cabin, and some even have baths."

"Loosh pools?" We could take a dip together.

A row of small cabins had been built beneath tall, broad columbisk trees with a dense forest behind. He led me toward the cute buildings, and I prayed he didn't notice I was staggering. Damn stasis. It should wear off anytime. Although, I savored the lack of sexual inhibition it gave me —a deficit my ex had pointed out one time too many.

Dekrin frowned, and his head tilted as he studied my

face. When his gaze drifted down my body, my nipples ached. "No one here needs loosh pools."

"I can see that."

"See what?"

"You wouldn't need anything to spark your fire." I couldn't miss something swelling beneath the front of his pants.

"This has to be the stasis talking," he groaned. "You're going to hate yourself when it finally wears off. You'll wake up later with a headache and a touch of mortification, and I'm telling you right now, I won't hold you to anything you've said since you arrived."

"What if I want you to hold me to it?"

His growl slipped out. "We need to get you to bed."

"We do," I said with a pert nod.

He guided my weaving body toward the cabin farthest on the right. They were cute, each constructed of real wood, something rarely seen on Earth, because we had to preserve our trees.

At the door, he placed his palm over the dualong . I'd heard of locks like this. Slightly sentient beings, they would remember the palm imprint of anyone allowed access.

He took my hand and held it over the square, and the device hummed, telling me it was now programmed to me.

A swipe of his fingers across the surface resulted in another hum.

"I've made sure it only gives you access."

"Do I need to lock my door to keep intruders out?" I teased my finger down his chest, salivating over each indent of muscle. "Maybe I'd like to invite a few of them in." Well, one of them, that is.

"I promise I'll forget," he said, his voice thready. He

yanked on his hair, dislodging the string used to hold it back. It flared across his shoulders in a silver-banded black wave, and I'd give almost anything to bury my face in the strands.

With a sigh, I turned in the open doorway, and when I started to list forward, he caught me with a firm grip on my upper arm.

His frustrated growl ripped from his chest. "I should leave you here. I need to leave you here. But I'm worried you'll fall."

With my head hopping around in the clouds, I couldn't tell what my body might do. The connection between them had been snipped, like I'd soon do with rogue vines.

"This doesn't mean anything," he said, scooping me up into his arms. He strode through the cozy living area with a tiny galley across the back and through a door on the left.

Ah, the bed awaited.

With my arms around his big broad shoulders, I looked up at his pretty face. Who woulda thought Nomir males could be this gorgeous? That was a vital detail the Intergalactic Employment Agency had left out.

"Would you pretty please," I half-slurped.

"Pretty please what?" He stopped beside the bed, his green eyes sparkling with humor. "You're really going to hate this conversation later."

"No, I'm..." I hiccupped and tried to ignore how my nipples beaded against his strong chest. I batted my eyelashes. "Would you pretty please join me in bed?"

One of his dark purple eyebrows lifted, and the battering ram in his pants surged upward, nudging the bottom of my butt.

"Not while you're under stasis," he said firmly, tossing

me onto the bed. "Get some sleep. You'll feel better later. I'll come back another time to show you around."

He pivoted on his heel and essentially raced from my cabin.

Pick up your copy of
Cultivating the Alien on Amazon.

www.ingramcontent.com/pod-product-compliance
Lightning Source LLC
Chambersburg PA
CBHW020321160726
47992CB00004B/1643